"Since you obviously aren't Nate Beaumont, who the hell are you?"

If he didn't know who she was, he couldn't have tracked her here. Unwillingly, Nicola turned her head so that they were face-to-face. Their bodies were pressed together intimately. As if they were lovers. She was no longer afraid of the man who'd pinned her to the ground in self-defense. She was very much aware of him—no longer as an enemy, but as a man.

"I'm not going to hurt you. I might even be able to help."

"Nicki Carson. Nicola, actually." She listened to her own voice with a sense of disbelief. She had intended to stay silent. But somehow the thought of having assistance— from this stranger—was just too tempting.

Dear Harlequin Intrigue Reader,

This month Harlequin Intrigue has an enthralling array of breathtaking romantic suspense to make the most of those last lingering days of summer.

The wait is finally over! The next crop of undercover agents who belong to the newest branch of the top secret Confidential organization are about to embark on an unbelievable adventure. Award-winning reader favorite Gayle Wilson will rivet you with the launch book of this brand-new ten-story continuity series. COLORADO CONFIDENTIAL will begin in Harlequin Intrigue, break out into a special release anthology and finish in Harlequin Historicals. In *Rocky Mountain Maverick*, an undeniably sexy undercover agent infiltrates a powerful senator's ranch and falls under the influence of an intoxicating impostor. Be there from the very beginning!

The adrenaline rush continues in *The Butler's Daughter* by Joyce Sullivan, with the first book in her new miniseries, THE COLLINGWOOD HEIRS. A beautiful guardian has been entrusted with the care of a toddler-sized heir, but now they are running for their lives and she must place their safety in an enigmatic protector's tantalizing hands! Ann Voss Peterson heats things up with *Incriminating Passion* when a targeted "witness" to a murder manages to inflame the heart of a by-the-book assistant D.A.

Finally rounding out the month is *Semiautomatic Marriage* by veteran author Leona Karr. Will the race to track down a killer culminate in a *real* trip down the aisle for an undercover husband and wife?

So pick up all four of these pulse-pounding stories and end the summer with a bang!

Sincerely,

Denise O'Sullivan
Harlequin Intrigue, Senior Editor

ROCKY MOUNTAIN MAVERICK

GAYLE WILSON

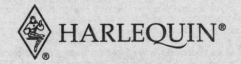

TORONTO • NEW YORK • LONDON
AMSTERDAM • PARIS • SYDNEY • HAMBURG
STOCKHOLM • ATHENS • TOKYO • MILAN • MADRID
PRAGUE • WARSAW • BUDAPEST • AUCKLAND

Special thanks and acknowledgment are given to
Gayle Wilson for her contribution to the
COLORADO CONFIDENTIAL series.

ISBN 0-373-22721-3

ROCKY MOUNTAIN MAVERICK

Visit us at www.eHarlequin.com

Printed in U.S.A.

ABOUT THE AUTHOR

Five-time RITA® Award finalist and RITA® Award winner Gayle Wilson has written twenty-seven novels and two novellas for Harlequin/Silhouette. She has won more than forty awards and nominations for her work. Recent recognitions include a 2002 Daphne du Maurier Award for Romantic Suspense.

Gayle still lives in Alabama, where she was born, with her husband of thirty-three years. She loves to hear from readers. Write to her at P.O. Box 3277, Hueytown, AL 35023. Visit Gayle online at http://suspense.net/gayle-wilson.

Books by Gayle Wilson

*Home to Texas
**Men of Mystery
†More Men of Mystery
‡Phoenix Brotherhood

The Confidential Code

COLORADO
CONFIDENTIAL

I will protect my country and its citizens.

I will stand in the line of fire
between innocents and criminals.

I will back up
my fellow agents without questions.

I will trust my instincts.

And most of all…

I WILL KEEP MY MISSION AND MY
IDENTITY STRICTLY CONFIDENTIAL

★★★★

CAST OF CHARACTERS

Colleen Wellesley—Colleen's first assignment as head of the newly organized Colorado Confidential is to find the kidnapped heir of the Langworthy empire. She soon discovers that the case she's been given involves far more than a missing baby....

Nicola Carson—An intern in Senator Franklin Gettys's Washington office, Nicki staged a disappearing act when she realized her life was in danger. Now, hiding in plain sight of her enemies, she tries to unravel the mystery behind why she became a target.

Michael Wellesley—Burned-out ex-CIA agent Michael Wellesley undertakes one last assignment as a favor for his sister and finds himself embroiled in a situation as perilous as any he's ever faced.

Charlie Quarrels—Foreman of the mysterious Half Spur ranch. Is Quarrels an innocent dupe or the mastermind of a diabolical experiment?

Ralph Mapes—The old man knows more about what's happening on the Half Spur than he should, but will he be willing to tell before it's too late?

For Emily,
who is smart, independent, feisty
and a bit of a maverick.
One day you'll make a great heroine
for your own hero—
just not too soon, please!

Prologue

It had happened several times in the past couple of weeks—an eerie, eyes-on-the-back-of-her-neck feeling. Often enough that whenever she was out in the city alone she had to resist the urge to keep glancing over her shoulder.

Nicola Carson couldn't quite put her finger on when or why that nervousness had begun. All she knew was that at one time she hadn't minded working late, even if the Senate Office Building was nearly deserted by the time she finished. Now she had to steel herself to face stepping out onto the nighttime streets of Washington, D.C.

And that's ridiculous, she told herself, as she hurried down the steps, holding the collar of her coat closed against her throat with one gloved hand. There was a hint of snow in the December air, making her homesick for the crisp, cold air of the Colorado Rockies where she'd grown up.

Which is also ridiculous. She was living her dream, working as an intern in the office of one of the most powerful men in the capital, and all she could think about lately was a life she once couldn't wait to leave behind.

Despite her pep talk, as she walked, heels clicking against the sidewalk with a quick, staccato rhythm, her uneasiness grew. *Don't look back. Don't look back.* She chanted the words in her mind, determined not to give in to this unreasonable paranoia.

She wouldn't have been out this late if Senator Gettys hadn't handed her a package as he was leaving and asked her to deliver it personally before she went home. She couldn't imagine why the disk she'd just left at the senator's campaign headquarters couldn't have been couriered over tomorrow, but it wasn't her place to ask those kinds of questions. It was her place to be as useful as possible.

Normally, she wouldn't have had any problem with anything she was assigned to do. She had no illusions about her role in the grand scheme of things. For someone who had grown up on a farm, helping with every unglamorous chore required to keep it running, she had never felt that any task was beneath her dignity.

She was grateful to be here. Grateful to have been chosen for an internship out of all the other applicants. Grateful for the opportunity to live in the nation's capital and participate in government at work.

Even as she repeated the litany, trying to bury her uneasiness in the enumeration of all the things she had to be thankful for, behind her—like an echo—came the sound of another set of footsteps. Her heart rate accelerated suddenly, and adrenaline pumped into her bloodstream in a gut-clenching rush.

The Metro entrance was half a block away. Surely, despite the cold, deserted streets around her, there would be someone there. At least there would be more light. Nothing ever seemed as frightening if you didn't have to face it in the darkness.

She increased her pace. By the time she reached the escalator that descended to the Metro, she was almost running. And none of the strategies she had used before against this insane panic seemed to be working.

She wanted to get on the train. Out of the darkness and among others who were leaving their offices late and heading home.

Hand on the rail, she clattered down the moving metal stairs, her own descent making so much noise that she couldn't possibly hear anything else. At the foot of the escalator, she turned and looked quickly toward the top.

There was nothing there. No one was following her. Maybe there had never been anyone behind her. No footsteps but her own, loud in the emptiness of the dark streets.

She took a breath in relief. Then, clutching her coat around her, she headed toward the platform.

She pressed her fare card against the red circle without really looking at it. *Almost there. Almost to the train. People. Safety.*

As she walked toward the track, the sound of her heels on the red, hexagonal tiles echoed and reechoed against the walls. This time she ignored the sound. After all, she knew there was no one behind her. And absolutely no cause for the sense of panic she had felt.

She breathed deeply, trying to calm the near hysteria that threatened. She could hear the train in the distance. Thankfully, despite the lateness of the hour and this less trafficked location, there were a few people waiting on the platform.

She was less than fifty feet from the track, the sound of the oncoming train was growing louder by the second. Her attention focused on the waiting passengers, all of whom were watching its approach, she caught a flicker of movement out of the corner of her eye.

Before she could turn to identify its source, a hand fastened onto the long strands of hair that spilled over the back of her coat. The pressure was strong enough not only to jerk her head backward and stop her forward motion, but to physically pull her in its direction.

Because it took too long to realize what was happening, a gloved hand fastened over her mouth before she could release the scream crowding her throat. Not that it would have made any difference. The train came ever closer, filling the waffle-weave concrete tunnel with noise.

Eyes watering from the pain, she clawed at the fingers over her lips. The hand that had grabbed her hair released to snake around her body, the forearm settling under her breasts.

Driven by panic, she increased her efforts to break out of her attacker's hold, futilely twisting and turning. She aimed a few kicks backward, but they never seemed to connect solidly with whoever was behind her.

There was no doubt in her mind it was a man. Not only was he stronger than she was, but given the angle at which he was holding her, he must top her own five foot ten inch height by a good two or three inches.

She knew by now that this wasn't a robbery. The strap of her purse had slipped off her shoulder in those first desperate moments. The purse had fallen to the floor, items rolling from it to clatter out onto the tile. He had ignored it completely, meaning…

She stopped prying at his fingers and began battering at his face with her fists. She couldn't see it, of course, and the blows, delivered above and behind her head, seemed to have as little effect as clawing at his hand had done.

Where the hell was security? The Metro was supposed to be safe, every area equipped with cameras to prevent attacks like this. Her eyes searched for the one that should cover this location. It was there, but for some reason, its lens was pointed away from the platform entry. By accident or design?

The train arrived, filling the station with noise, and the fingers that had been fastened over her mouth began to move. So that he could put both hands around her throat? Or to allow him to take out a weapon?

A knife? Oh, my God, not a knife.

In the endless seconds she fought, her imagination conjured up every urban horror story she had ever heard, playing them in her head like a tape running on fast forward. In desperation, she bent her knees, lifting her feet off the ground and letting her full weight pull against his hold.

For a split second, as he tried to counteract that move, she would be out of his control. She knew that was all she would have. A split second to decide her own fate.

Everything seemed to happen at once, yet each movement, each breath, each heartbeat was etched with complete clarity on her brain. As she'd anticipated, his body began to shift in an attempt to maintain his balance. He tried to set her on her feet, but in order to do that, he had to bend forward, negating the advantage his height had given him.

Before he could straighten away, Nicola put her feet back on the ground and used the muscles in her thighs and buttocks, strengthened by years of horseback riding, to propel her body upward. The top of her head collided with the man's chin, striking so hard that she heard his teeth snap together.

And hard enough that the air thinned and darkened around her. She fought to stay conscious as she staggered forward like a drunk.

Behind her she heard something metallic clatter against the tile. The knife she had thought he was reaching for?

Her purse lay directly in her path. She bent, scooping it up by the strap without slowing. Ahead of her the doors of the train car were beginning to close.

The same fear that had driven her to use her skull as a weapon drove her in a sprint toward them, determined that they wouldn't close her out, leaving her trapped on a deserted subway platform with a madman.

She wedged her arm between the doors, forcing her shoulder through as the rubber-lined edges began to close against her body. She didn't stop to consider whether or not she could pry them open enough to get in. There was no choice. This was life or death, and she didn't want to die.

Dear God, she didn't want to die.

Her body slid through the narrowing opening as the doors closed with a whoosh. Panting from exertion and terror, she leaned against them, trembling, her eyes squeezed tight against the threat of tears.

And then she opened them, knowing there was something she still had to do. She turned, looking through the window behind her as the train gathered speed.

The emptiness of the platform was broken only by shadows cast by the grill-encased lights above it. There was no sign of the man who had attacked her.

A man who had known exactly where to find her. A man who had had that information in time to push the security camera out of alignment.

And there was only one person who could have told him. They would try again, she realized. Unless…

She closed her mouth, aware for the first time that her breath was sawing in and out, loud enough to be audible over the noise of the train. The woman in the seat across the aisle was staring at her, eyes wide with shock.

Nicki bent her head, gathering control. She realized that she still held the strap of her purse in her hand. She lifted the soft, leather bag, fumbling inside it with her left hand until her fingers closed over the familiar shape of her bill-fold.

She didn't have to go back to her apartment. Never again

would she go back there. Or anywhere else he might expect her to be. She had everything she needed right here, she thought, her hand resting protectively over the wallet that contained her ticket to safety.

Her upbringing had taught her the value of money. She had saved as much as she could, carefully putting part of what she made into her savings account every month. All of it was accessible through any of the thousands of ATM machines in this city.

There was enough there. Enough to get her somewhere far away from here. Far enough to be safe.

Please, God, let somewhere be far enough for that.

Chapter One

I hope to hell Frost was right and home is *the place where they have to take you in,* Michael Wellesley thought as he pulled the SUV he'd bought in Denver into the circular drive. It wasn't really that he had nowhere else to go, but the Royal Flush was home. It always would be.

He had realized that anew as he'd driven across the river, his stomach tightening in anticipation of his first glimpse of the house and the barn. *Home.*

Like a beaten dog, he was returning to his birthplace to lick his wounds. At least that's what Colleen would think.

And what if she did? He had a right to be here, despite what his father had done.

He could now think about the provision in his dad's will, the one that had given the family ranch to Colleen, without the bitterness and anger that had driven him away at eighteen. He still wondered, however, why his father had done something that seemed so grossly unfair.

Maybe to force him to make it on his own. To become a man. His own man. Or maybe, Michael had finally decided, because he had never told anyone, much less his father, how much he had loved this place. That had obviously been a mistake.

He shut off the ignition and opened the car door, easing

down carefully from the high seat. As he'd expected, his knee had stiffened, both from the long flight and the hours he'd spent behind the wheel.

Right hand on the top of the door, left on the roof for support, he took an experimental step, testing it. Prepared for the pain, he managed to control his response to it except for a slight tightening of his lips and a nearly soundless inhalation.

It would have been smart to bring the cane, if only for the duration of the trip. Instead, he'd tossed it into one of the trash bins outside Reagan. Just as he'd metaphorically trashed everything else associated with the past eight years of his life.

Still holding on to the top of the door as he flexed the damaged knee, Michael allowed his gaze to scan the compound. The place looked prosperous and well kept. Both the barn and the house had been freshly painted. He had already noted that the grazing stock he passed on the way in from the highway were sleek and healthy. Maybe his father had known what he was doing after all.

Rejecting that thought, he stepped away from the door, slamming it behind him. Limping heavily, he walked around to the rear, opening the door there to drag out his duffel bag.

He'd stuffed every item of clothing from his wardrobe that might be appropriate for the ranch into it. And he'd been surprised by how little of that there was. The rest, with exception of a couple of suits hanging from a hook in the back seat, he'd given away.

He closed the hatch, the noise unnaturally loud in the drowsy afternoon heat. He'd half expected someone to come out by now to investigate the arrival of a strange car.

Of course, it was possible there was no one in the main house. There were always a hundred things that needed seeing to on a ranch this size, especially in the middle of summer.

He walked around the car and up the low steps, boot heels echoing across the wooden planks of the porch. Switching the duffel bag to his left hand, he raised his right to punch the bell.

Somewhere in the back of his mind the word "home" echoed. He changed the motion he'd begun, his fingers fastening around the knob instead. He opened the door, letting it swing inward to a cool dimness.

At the far end of the huge central room it revealed, the brass fittings on the old bar, a survivor from the days when the Royal Flush had been the fanciest bordello in Colorado, caught the late afternoon light. Michael's eyes lifted automatically, searching for the portrait of his great-great-grandmother, which had always hung behind it.

Old Dora was still there. It seemed nothing about the Flush had changed. Of course, it never had.

He set the duffel bag down on the rich, heart pine floor and stood in the somnolent stillness, letting the memories close around him. As he did, he became aware of voices coming from behind the house. One was obviously male. And the other…

Colleen? If so, it might be easier for both of them if their first meeting took place outside. At least then she wouldn't have to throw him out of the house.

His lips tilted at the image. At maybe five foot five to his six-three, she'd play hell trying. Of course, a challenge, even one of that proportion, had never discouraged his sister.

He realized he was anticipating seeing her again, just as he'd been looking forward to his first sight of the house from the moment he'd turned off Highway 9. Whatever bitterness he'd felt toward his father had never extended to Colleen. Or, if it had then, it certainly didn't now.

In the nearly sixteen years since he'd been here, he'd been to hell and back. The only family he'd known in all that time had been the men who had fought and died beside him. Without that bond—

Deliberately he broke the thought. Today wasn't about guilt or regret. Today was about homecoming. And the sooner he got this one over with, the better for everyone concerned.

"ALL I'M TELLING YOU—"

"And all I'm telling *you* is to handle it," Colleen interrupted. "That's what I pay you for, Dex."

"Why don't you just sell the damn place to someone who'll appreciate it?"

"*I* appreciate it. That doesn't mean I want to be in on every minor decision of its day-to-day operation."

"What I'm asking you about isn't minor, Colleen. And you damn well know it."

"I also know you'll make the right decision, with or without my advice. I'm not real sure why you're so all-fired set on having it."

Michael had already heard enough to identify the man his sister was arguing with as her foreman. And anger was apparent in each muscular inch of the man's body. It was also apparent that those muscles were not the kind built in a gym, but through the hard, backbreaking work a ranch demanded.

Besides, he had the look of a cowboy, both in his tall, rangy build and sun-darkened skin. It was obvious that, boss-lady or not, Colleen did not intimidate him.

"You don't deserve what you've got," the foreman said, his voice no longer raised. It was quiet and somehow far more effective at expressing his disgust. He ran a hand through black hair that had a liberal sprinkling of gray. "Maybe because you had this place handed to you on a silver platter, you think it don't require any work on your part to keep it."

Colleen took a breath, her lips tight, visibly controlling her own temper. Although it had been a decade or more since he'd seen her, Michael had had no trouble recognizing his sister. She had the Wellesley coloring, of course. Dark brown hair and those strange blue-green eyes that a few women in his past had unfortunately referred to as turquoise.

Whatever color they were, it looked a whole hell of a lot better on Colleen. She was still a good-looking woman, despite the fact that she must be...

When he'd done the math, he realized with a sense of shock that his sister was forty-five. Nine years older than he, she had been only twenty-nine when he'd joined the military.

A lifetime ago. A lifetime he knew almost nothing about.

"I work," she said, her tone as intense as that of the man who'd made the accusation. "And damned hard, too. What I do makes it possible for this operation to survive no matter how the markets fluctuate. Just because I don't want to be consulted about every little detail doesn't give you the right to suggest I don't appreciate the Flush."

"Then act like it, damn it."

"If you're trying to convince her to do something," Michael said, choosing that moment to reveal himself by stepping out of the shadows from where he'd been watching the confrontation, "I can tell you for a fact that you'll fare better not cussing her. Gets her back up every time."

With his first word, their heads had snapped toward him,

almost in unison. Two pairs of eyes—one hostile and suspicious, the other slightly narrowed—focused on him.

"Who the hell are you?" the cowboy demanded.

"Michael." Colleen breathed his name as if she couldn't believe what she was seeing.

Because he had been watching for her reaction—a matter of training as well as need—he had known the exact instant when she'd accepted her identification. What was in her eyes as she did eased tensions he hadn't been aware he harbored.

"Hello, Colleen. It's been a long time."

She shook her head, her eyes welling with tears. She fought them, succeeding only because she was determined and because whatever his sister set her mind to, she accomplished. When she was again in control, she turned to the man with whom she'd been arguing.

"Dex, if you'll excuse me. We can talk about this later, please. Right now I have some...unfinished business I need to take care of."

"Something more important than the ranch?" Dex asked, his voice edged with bitterness.

Colleen turned to smile at Michael, ignoring the taunt. "Much more important," she said softly.

The cowboy's hazel eyes locked briefly with his. Michael inclined his head as if they had been introduced. A muscle in the other man's jaw knotted, but he didn't make any further objection. He slammed the battered Stetson he'd held in his right hand back on his head and stalked off.

Colleen didn't even glance his way, her eyes examining Michael's face as if she were trying to memorize it.

"I can't believe you're here."

"I hope you don't mind."

"*Mind?* God, Michael, you have to know better than that."

A little more of the tension seeped out of his body at the sincerity of her exclamation. She reinforced it by stepping forward and holding both her hands out to him. After a second's hesitation, he put his into hers, using them to pull her against his body in an awkward embrace.

It didn't remain awkward for long. Colleen leaned against him, her arms fastening around his waist in a fierce hug. Almost against his will, Michael found himself responding to that honest emotion.

After a moment she stepped away to look up into his eyes. Hers were once more suspiciously touched with moisture, but she was smiling.

"I wish I could tell you how wonderful you look, but, truth be told—"

"I look like hell," he finished for her.

"Are you okay?"

The depth of concern in her voice was almost his undoing. He hated that emotion seemed so near the surface now, but the idiot shrink the agency had insisted he talk to had told him he could expect that. Maybe so, but that didn't mean he had to like it.

"I will be," he said, forcing a smile. Her lips quickly answered it, but her eyes were still clouded. Slightly anxious. "I thought I might hang out here for a while. If I won't be in the way."

For one instant there was a flicker of something in the blue-green depths of her eyes. It was gone before he could even think about identifying what he'd seen. Her smile broadened immediately, and she leaned forward to kiss him on the cheek.

"Welcome home, little brother," she said. "And when you're all rested up, there are a couple of paint ponies that could use some schooling. Think you're up to that?"

"I will be," Michael promised, and for the first time in nearly six months, he began to believe that might be true.

"GUILTY OR NOT, Cal Demarco's still a son of a bitch."

Michael could hear the anger in Colleen's voice despite the nearly ten years that had passed since the Internal Affairs Division of the Denver Police Department had cleared her former supervisor of the corruption charges she'd leveled against him.

"Unfortunately, they don't put you away for that," he said, "or jails would be a whole lot more crowded than they are now."

The bourbon his sister had been pouring with a generous hand had finally eased the ever-present ache in his knee. It had also served to destroy any sense of strain his long absence might have caused between them.

"I could suggest a few other candidates." She lifted her glass, resting it against her chin as she considered him. She was sitting on the couch opposite his, legs curled under her. "And now that I've caught you up on the sad, uninteresting story of my life, I think it's time to hear what you've been up to."

He hesitated, thinking about what he wanted to tell her, as well as what he couldn't. Most of that was for security reasons, but some he just didn't want to talk about.

"Suffice it to say that I'm retired."

Her lips pursed, her eyes still on his face. "From the military."

It hadn't been phrased as a question, but he nodded, dropping his eyes to the amber liquid he was absently swirling in the bottom of his glass. He lifted it, anticipating the dark, smoky bite of his grandfather's private stock.

"Except you left the Rangers more than eight years ago."

His hand halted in midmotion as his eyes jumped up to meet hers.

"I'm just curious what you've been doing since," she said. "Or is that privileged information?"

He didn't answer, holding her gaze as silent seconds ticked by.

"You're the only family I have left, Michael. It's unlikely I wouldn't try to find out where you were and what you were doing."

What was unlikely, he thought, was that she could have.

"And did you?"

"That surprises you."

"Considering."

She smiled at him, seeming pleased she'd been able to shock him. "I know you worked for Jack Waigner up until December of last year. I don't know where you've been for the last six months. You...dropped off my radar screen."

Her eyes briefly touched on the knee she'd pointedly avoided asking him about, in spite of its obvious impairment.

"Hospital and then rehab," he said. That, too, was probably obvious, given what she already knew.

"That's why you retired?" This time her acknowledgment of the injury he'd suffered was more open, her eyes tracing along the long, blue-jean clad length of his leg, stretched out on the coffee table between them.

Was it? That wasn't a question he'd allowed himself to think too much about.

"Partially."

"I've thought about the timing of your disappearance. About what was going on then. Wondering if there was a connection."

"And you think you've figured it out," he said flatly, reading confidence in her tone.

"I asked some questions."

"And got *answers?*" he asked, his voice deliberately quizzical.

He hadn't quite been able to put together how, living here, his sister could know things no one outside the intelligence community *should* know. Nor had he figured out where her questions were headed. He'd be willing to bet, however, that this conversation wasn't about familial concern. Nor was it the product of an idle curiosity.

"A few. Enough, I think. San Parrano maybe," she suggested.

The words evoked memories he never wanted to think about again. He had worked hard on erasing the nightmare images from what had been a joint Special Forces/CIA counterterrorist mission. One that had gone very wrong very quickly.

"You were there, weren't you?"

He nodded, then raised the glass and tossed down the last swallow of liquor. It burned a path along the back of his throat, despite the ache that had formed there.

"And you don't want to talk about it."

"I don't want to *think* about it," he said truthfully. He leaned forward, setting the empty glass down on the coffee table.

"I understand Waigner sent his best people."

"Most of them died. Hardly a recommendation."

"I don't know. It's good enough for me."

The small smile was back, but he couldn't quite read it. A little self-satisfied. Maybe even challenging. In response, he tilted his head, raising his brows in inquiry.

"I could use some help right now," she said, "and since you're here…"

Get up now, he told himself. *Walk down the hall to your bedroom, thoughtfully located on the ground floor. Crawl into bed, pull the covers over your head, and pretend this conversation never happened.*

"Help with what?" he said instead.

"An assignment."

After she'd left the police department, Colleen had set up her own private investigation agency. She ran it from behind the scenes, and from what she'd told him earlier, it had become very successful.

This offer to join it was probably her way of getting him back on his feet, as misguided as the idea was. He'd been approached by other people with the same purpose during the last couple of months. His answer hadn't been repeatable. He mitigated his response to his sister, however, because he truly believed she acted out of love.

"I'm no P.I., but thanks for the thought."

"You think I'm patronizing you."

He smiled rather than responding with what he thought.

"I really do need your help, Michael. I'm assuming your security clearances are all in order."

"For what it's worth."

"A baby's life," she said softly. "What would *that* be worth to you?"

Chapter Two

Every time he thought he'd figured out where this was going, Colleen threw him a curve. He didn't much like this last one. "Whose baby?"

"Samuel Langworthy's grandson."

Even as he'd asked the question, Michael had realized there was only one baby who'd occupied the headlines of the nation's newspapers during the past two weeks. He'd read stories back in Virginia about the Langworthy kidnapping. The coverage here in Colorado had probably been ten times as intense, not only because of the political ramifications, but because it involved one of the founding families of the state.

The Langworthys were Colorado's version of the Kennedys, and to most people here they were every bit as glamorous. Samuel, the patriarch, had served as governor. His run at the Senate had been interrupted by heart trouble, so his political dreams were being lived out by his son, Joshua.

A Harvard Law grad who had come home to work for the Department of Justice, Josh Langworthy was currently running for governor. There were also two Langworthy daughters, but Michael had been away from the state too long to remember their names.

"Langworthy hired you?"

"Not Langworthy," Colleen said. "This is…something official."

"Meaning what?"

He wondered for a moment if she'd maintained some connection to the Denver police. That wouldn't explain, of course, how she had known so much about what he had been doing for the past eight years.

"ICU has been recruited."

Investigations, Confidential & Undercover was Colleen's agency, which she'd started after she left the police force. Who might have "recruited" a private investigation firm and to do what was another question.

One he refused to ask. She seemed to want to tell this in her own way. He had plenty of time to listen.

"You probably don't remember Dad's friend, Mitch Forbes."

"From Texas?"

Colleen nodded and leaned forward to refill his glass. When she had, she held it out to him across the table. As he reached for it, she said, "He asked me to organize a branch of the investigative arm of the Department of Public Safety here in Colorado, just as he's done in Texas. Something called Colorado Confidential."

"I'm not sure I follow. To investigate what?"

"Threats to the public safety," she said, as if that explained everything. "On a local level, of course."

"And the Langworthy baby's kidnapping qualifies as a threat to public safety?" He didn't bother to mask his skepticism.

"Someone in DPS thinks so."

"And that's good enough for you?"

"Did you question Jack Waigner when he sent you to San Parrano?"

"I should have."

She smiled, recognizing the gallows humor for what it was.

"I don't question my orders either. I try to carry them out to the best of my ability. And frankly, you'd be a real asset right now in helping me accomplish that."

"I think that would be a matter of opinion."

"Yes, it is. Mine. All I'm asking is that you sit in on a meeting. Offer suggestions. Criticisms. Maybe undertake a little legwork." Again her eyes touched on his knee. "Whatever you feel up to."

If there was anything more likely to get him to agree than that note of unctuous concern in his sister's voice, he couldn't imagine what it would be.

"Anybody ever tell you that you don't play fair?" he said, letting her know that he recognized what she was doing.

"I play to win," she said. "And I make no apologies for it."

"EVERYONE, this is my brother, Michael. I've asked him to join us today to offer suggestions and observations." As she talked, Colleen's eyes touched on the face of each of the three people gathered around the table.

During last night's tour, she had shown Michael the renovations she'd made that allowed Colorado Confidential to function efficiently from the ranch. The room where they were meeting today, its entrance cleverly hidden behind a wine rack, had once been the basement storage area. Beyond this room, behind another disguised entrance, a second room contained state-of-the-art surveillance equipment, which, he admitted, nearly rivaled that of the CIA.

"And in case you're wondering," she went on, "his security clearances are higher than mine."

There was a nearly imperceptible change in the atmosphere. A relaxation, perhaps, now that his presence had been explained. And a curiosity that was expressed to varying degrees in the three pairs of eyes, all of which had settled on him. Evaluating.

He was more than willing to play the role of consultant, but he had no interest in getting involved in any fieldwork. As slow as he was right now, he'd be a hazard to the rest of the team.

"I didn't know you had a brother." The comment sounded vaguely sympathetic, perhaps because it came from the only female member of the group.

"Fiona Clark," Colleen said, introducing the woman who'd spoken. "Ex-FBI. From Chicago."

"It's nice to meet you." Small, blond and delicate, Clark didn't look or sound like anyone's idea of an FBI agent, which had undoubtedly been to her advantage.

"Shawn Jameson. Arson investigator, currently employed at the Royal Flush. From…?"

"Around," Jameson said. His blue eyes mocked the relevance of Colleen's question.

Without seeming the least bit embarrassed by his lack of response, she turned to the last of the three operatives at the table.

"And this is Night Walker. Former bounty hunter and private security specialist. Night works with the horse-breeding operation here on the ranch. Among other things."

Both the name and the long, raven's-wing black hair indicated Walker's heritage. As far as Michael was concerned, the fact that Colleen had hired him to handle her beloved horses said all he needed to know about the man's character.

"I'm sure most of you know about the Langworthy kidnapping. With the media coverage, it would be pretty hard not to. Colorado Confidential has been asked to conduct its own investigation, since the official one seems to be going nowhere. And, more importantly, since there are some aspects of the case that set off alarm bells in Washington.''

"Can you tell us what those are?" Shawn asked.

"They haven't told me," Colleen admitted. "Just that, like other things we've handled for the Department of Public Safety in the last six months, there's more to this abduction than meets the eye. We'll be working closely with the head of the Colorado DPS, Wiley Longbottom, on a need-to-know basis. We've been told enough to determine some initial avenues of investigation. That's our first order of business. To decide who does what.''

A little more democratic than what Michael was accustomed to, but no one seemed to find it strange that they were being let in on the decision making.

"As you know, Schyler Langworthy, three months old, was taken from his crib in the Langworthy's home in Denver on the night of the Fourth of July. It happened while the family was attending a campaign rally for Josh Langworthy, who is currently a candidate for governor."

"I think we all know the history on this," Fiona Clark offered, obviously in an attempt to cut short the background.

"I wasn't sure that Michael did," Colleen explained.

Again, three pairs of eyes focused on him. Since his sister had covered most of this with him last night, Michael believed she had some other agenda for this rehash of things they all knew. He was willing to serve as her excuse.

"Samuel Langworthy thinks Governor Houghton and Senator Gettys are somehow involved, maybe in hopes that the kidnapping will distract Josh from the campaign. I'm not sure that belief is based on anything other than the political bad blood that exists between the three. Considering the seriousness of the accusation, however, Houghton and Gettys have been questioned. Discretely questioned, given their positions. The governor suggested that the kidnapping is a desperate move on the part of the Langworthy clan to gain a sympathy vote for Josh's flagging campaign.''

"I thought he was ahead in the polls," Shawn said.

"Not according to the opposition's *private* polls. Who knows where the race really stands? However, according to our sources, Langworthy—that's Samuel, not Josh—also hasn't been completely forthcoming with the authorities. The agents who questioned him felt he might know more about his grandson's disappearance than he told them. Given who he is, they couldn't act on their feelings, of course.''

"Meaning no bright lights and rubber hoses for the head of the Colorado's Centennial Family," Fiona suggested lightly.

"Meaning Langworthy is still a very powerful and respected name in this state. Whatever investigation of the family we undertake must also be discreet. *Very* discreet.''

Michael's gaze had been drawn to Night Walker, maybe because he was the only one who hadn't offered an opinion or a suggestion. However, there seemed to be some spark of animation in those dark eyes now that hadn't been there when the former bounty hunter had been introduced.

"That's why I thought Night might be the ideal candidate to conduct that part of the operation.''

There was no reaction to Colleen's words in Walker's impassive features.

"You once worked at the house," Colleen continued, as if his lack of response had been expected. "I think the baby's mother, Holly Langworthy, bears watching. If the Langworthys are involved, it's possible she may lead us to the baby. After all, her stake in this is higher than anyone else's. Except for the baby's father, of course. And no one seems to know who he is.''

There was some nuance of inflection in the last that Michael couldn't decode. Whatever it was, it had the desired effect. Night Walker nodded his agreement, a single up and down motion of his head.

''Good,'' Colleen said, glancing down at the sheet of paper on the desk in front of her. ''Fiona, that leaves Houghton and Gettys for you. Gettys's ex-wife might be a way to hone in on whatever shady dealings the senator's involved in.''

''You think there are some?'' Fiona asked. ''Shady dealings, I mean.''

''They've been rumored for years.''

''Nobody at that level of politics is ever completely clean,'' Shawn Jameson said. ''So where does that leave me? There doesn't seem to be another side in this nasty little war.''

''Well, I *do* need someone to check out a sheep farm that Gettys owns part of, but actually, I was hoping—''

''A sheep farm?'' Fiona broke in. ''You just lost me, Colleen. How does a sheep farm play into this?''

''Maybe you should have let me finish the intro,'' Colleen said, smiling to indicate her comment wasn't intended as a rebuke. ''One of the strangest aspects of the kidnapping was the trace evidence recovered from the baby's room.''

''Don't tell me,'' Shawn said, controlling an upward quirk at the corners of his mouth.

Colleen ignored him, again referring to her notes. ''Fibers identified as Merino wool were found on the bedding, along with particles of eggshell and dirt.'' She looked up, eyes again scanning the faces of the people at the table.

"The dirt, by the way, came from the southern part of the state."

"Egg shells and *wool?*" Fiona's question probably expressed what they were all feeling.

Colleen lifted her hands, palms upward. "All I can tell you is what the technicians found. And that Senator Gettys does own part of a sheep ranch somewhere in the mountains around Granby. It's a stretch, but enough of a coincidence that it seems worth checking out. Maybe just by having someone work there for a few weeks to see if there's anything remotely suspicious going on. The problem is...I have a couple of other leads DPS is working up. I had hoped to keep you here," she said to Shawn, "until something comes through on those."

No one said anything, although it must be obvious to them, as it was to him, what Colleen was hinting for. And she could hint until the cows came home, Michael decided. He wasn't getting back into covert operations. Especially not on some damn sheep farm. The assignment was obviously make-work, designed to give him something useful to do—something not too challenging, of course—and they both knew it.

The strained silence built until Jameson broke it, his eyes considering Michael. "If you want someone to hire on as a hand, maybe I should do it."

Michael knew exactly what had prompted that offer. The son of a bitch thought he wasn't up to working on a ranch. After all, Colleen's three hotshots had already been seated at the table when he'd limped into the room.

"You know a cowboy worth his keep who hasn't had a couple of broken bones?" he asked.

It was the first time he'd spoken, and no one seemed particularly eager to answer his question. Fiona's eyes fell to examine her hands, which were clasped together on top of the table.

Michael Wellesley couldn't remember the last time anyone had doubted his competence. With more than a dozen years of combined special ops and intel experience, some of it in places these three probably couldn't find on a map even if they'd heard of them, he wasn't about to let someone start now.

He might be beat up and battered, both mentally and physically, but the day he couldn't ride a horse or mend fence or herd some frigging sheep well enough to earn his keep, he'd quit. Not until. And that decision, when it came, sure as hell wasn't going to be made by someone else.

"If you're worried about Michael being able—"

"I'll do it," he said, his voice overriding his sister's attempted defense of his abilities.

It wasn't that he didn't know he'd been played. Or didn't understand that this was exactly what she'd been hoping for. And he did see the irony in his leaping into something he'd sworn he would never be involved in again.

Hell, he needed a success. Something to go right so that the long years of service to his country wouldn't end with that fiasco in San Parrano.

Besides, how hard could checking out a sheep farm be? It would do him good to work a few weeks in the open. He could use the time to get back into shape. To work on getting his head screwed back on straight. After all, it wasn't as if something really dangerous was likely to come up during Colleen's "therapy" assignment. Not likely at all.

Chapter Three

"This way each of the hands gets his own place," Charlie Quarrels said, as he unlocked the door of the small trailer to which he'd driven Michael. "Privacy. Folks these days seem to prefer that rather than all bedding down in a bunkhouse."

Despite the fact that he had the skills required for this job, Michael had been surprised at how quickly he'd been hired. The questions Quarrels had asked during his interview had been cursory. Michael's answers had been accepted at face value.

Now officially an employee, he was being given the grand tour of the Half Spur. Not that there was anything remotely grand about what he'd seen so far.

Employees lived in trailers that were scattered around the outer perimeter of the central compound. Judging by the interior of this one, he decided after he followed the foreman up the high step and then inside, none of them were living in luxury. Heated by propane and lighted by an outside generator, the small metal caravans would be freezing in winter and like ovens in a summer like this.

He'd been given the trailer farthest from the complex where the offices and shearing pens were located because, Quarrels had explained, Michael had his own transportation. Not the SUV, of course. He'd left that at the Royal Flush and purchased the most disreputable looking pickup he could find to make the journey north.

"Meals are down at the main cabin," the foreman went on. "Six, noon and six."

He assumed the main cabin referred to the building where his interview had been conducted. Michael had gotten the impression that some of the workers, including the foreman, lived on the premises. Everybody else got one of the trailers.

"I'll introduce you to the rest of 'em during supper. We're shorthanded right now, so there ain't all that many names to remember."

"Thanks," Michael said, swinging his duffel bag onto the narrow bed.

Little more than a cot, it didn't look as if it would be long enough to accommodate his height. Ever since he'd entered the trailer, he'd felt as if he needed to duck his head to avoid bumping the low ceiling. When this was over, Colleen was going to owe him big time.

"You can ride back down with me," Quarrels offered. "Ain't no need to start 'til morning. We'll be taking blood samples then."

"Blood samples?"

"This ain't just a sheep ranch. It's a government research facility."

Each syllable in the last two words had been enunciated separately, as if Quarrels had had to practice until he got the phrase right. Michael didn't ask what they were researching. He doubted the normal hired hand would give a damn, so that was the attitude he needed to adopt.

He'd had a lot of experience adapting to whatever role he was playing. Someone who couldn't bury himself

completely in a situation wasn't going to survive undercover work.

To him, that had always been one of its biggest draws—
the tension created by the dichotomy of disappearing into
a persona while maintaining the necessary vigilance about
who you really were and why you were there. It created a
constant adrenaline rush. Or as near to one as he had believed he could get.

"You ready?"

Michael turned to nod, but Quarrels hadn't waited for his
answer. He was already going down the steps that led to
the ground. Michael followed to find him standing at the
bottom of them, watching his descent with interest.

"Horse or a bull?" Quarrels asked, obviously referring
to his knee.

"Something like that," Michael said shortly, limping
around the dusty pickup to climb in on the passenger side.

"The cold up here in the winter plays hell with broke
bones." Quarrels started the truck, again seeming to expect
no answer.

"How many hands on the place?" Michael asked.

"Two permanent. Bunk in the cabin."

"Permanent?" Michael asked, wondering how the foreman made the classification.

"Been here more 'an a couple of years. Don't many stay
that long. Too isolated. No bright lights."

No lights at all, Michael thought, remembering Quarrels'
explanation about the generator's limited hours of operation.

As they talked, the pickup rattled over the dirt road that
led back down to the main cabin, which appeared to be the
center of the ranching operation. The speed at which it was
driven made no concession to the potholed roughness of
the track.

"Five temps, including you," Quarrels continued after a contemplative silence. "Ain't but a couple of them been here more 'an six months. Pays all right for what little you gotta do, but the place itself gets to people."

Yet it would have been difficult to find a more beautiful location. The magnificent Rockies loomed in the background. Abundant water from the spring runoff guaranteed the lush richness of the pastures. So far, Michael realized, he hadn't seen a single sheep.

Quarrels roared around the last curve with a shower of gravel, pulling the truck into the yard outside the main cabin. A man stood in its open doorway. His eyes, narrowed against the smoke wafting upward from the cigarette he held cupped in his hand, followed the two of them as they got out of the pickup and walked across the expanse of worn, patchy grass.

"Sal Johnson," Quarrels said, indicating the man in the door with a forward motion of his head. "This here's McAdams. What'd you say your first name was?"

"Mac'll do," Michael said, nodding to the cowboy with the cigarette.

Small and wiry, Johnson looked like dozens of other hands he'd known growing up. Skin burned to a wrinkled mahogany by a combination of wind and sun. Eyes perpetually squinted against its glare, even when it wasn't in the sky. Body stripped of every ounce of fat by the work he did.

"Pleased to meet'cha." Johnson threw the stub of his cigarette into the yard and stepped back, making room for them to come by him.

The central room of the cabin was the office, dominated by a battered old desk piled high with circulars and paperwork. Quarrels led the way through it, entering the hallway to the living quarters. There were three bedrooms off the hall, two on one side and one on the other, Quarrels pointed out as they passed the closed doorways.

The dining room at the end of the passage held one long table. The bar behind it was topped by a service window to the kitchen.

There a heavyset man, cigarette dangling from his lips, stirred something in a metal pot. He made no acknowledgment of their presence, despite the sound their boots made on the wooden floor.

"Still early," Quarrels said, heading for the seat at the end of the table.

Rank hath its privilege, Michael thought, amused by that assumption of power. He hesitated a moment, wondering if the other places were also spoken for.

"You can sit anywhere," the foreman advised, ending that speculation.

Michael deliberately chose a seat in the middle of the far side of the table, knowing, even as he did so, that most people would probably have sat down on the nearer side. He wanted to watch the rest of the hands assemble, however. To have a chance to observe them before they were aware they'd been joined by a newcomer.

Johnson, the one who'd been standing in the doorway when they arrived, entered the dining hall almost as soon as Michael sat down, followed closely by an older cowboy. That man extended his hand across the table before he took his seat.

"Ralph Mapes."

"McAdams," Michael said. "Call me Mac."

A metal bell tolled somewhere outside, interrupting the brief conversation.

"Warning bell," Quarrels said. "Means you got three minutes before cook serves it up."

Michael nodded. Johnson took a saltine out of the narrow

basket in the middle of the table, chewing it with serious concentration. Nobody else said anything. After a minute or so a group of four entered almost at the same time, settling rapidly into the remaining places at the table.

None of them introduced themselves as Mapes had done. And none of them paid him any overt attention. There were a couple of sidelong glances, eyes skating quickly away if they made contact with his.

The last person to enter was a lanky kid who looked as if he couldn't be more than eighteen or nineteen. By the time he got to the table, the only available chair was next to Michael. The boy slipped into it almost furtively, as if he expected someone to object.

His arrival seemed to be the signal. The cook, cigarette still between his lips, appeared, holding the metal pan by its handle. He set it down on the edge of the table and began ladling chili con carne from it into the bowls stacked in front of Quarrels.

As each was filled, it was passed along the table. A couple of the hands had picked up their spoons, holding them while they awaited their portion. Everyone began eating as soon as he was served.

Passing each serving to the kid beside him gave Michael an opportunity to observe him. His hands, visible as they took the bowls, bore silent witness to the work he did.

The knuckles were scuffed and reddened. Grime was embedded in the creases and around the rims of ragged nails. The plaid shirt he wore looked too large, with the ends of the cuffs resting low on the back of his hands.

The boy kept his eyes downcast, focused on the contents of the dishes he accepted. He never once looked up at the stranger beside him. Although the bowls were brimming with hot chili, there was something about his studied disinterest that seemed peculiar. Especially in a kid.

Almost all that was visible of him was a droop of long, mouse-colored hair, which hung down over his eyes and ears, and the rounded curve of a cheek. As Michael watched, a slow flood of color moved under the tanned skin, revealing that the boy knew he was being observed.

Based on what he saw, Michael revised his original estimate of the kid's age downward a couple of years. Runaway? he wondered.

This would certainly be the ideal hiding place for someone who was determined not to be found. And it was always possible it wasn't the kid's parents that he was hiding from. Men dodging warrants frequently joined that itinerate brotherhood who followed seasonal work across the West.

Quarrels hadn't inquired too closely into his credentials this afternoon. Based on Michael's previous experience with ranch hands, there were probably at least a couple seated at this table who couldn't afford any scrutiny from law enforcement. Running fingerprints from this bunch might prove to be an interesting exercise.

Despite his conviction that Colleen had sent him out here as some kind of occupational therapy, he realized that he was beginning to take this assignment seriously. Hardly surprising, since ''seriously'' had always been the only way he knew how to operate.

He turned to pass the last bowl to the boy. Only when he had did he realize the kid was already bent low over his serving of chili, spooning it into his mouth with a rapidity that spoke of real hunger.

As Michael held out the bowl, the kid turned to look at it before he finally raised his eyes to Michael's face. The deep, clear blue of a summer sky, they locked on his for maybe two seconds before they were returned to the serious business of eating.

The force of their impact, however, had been like an

electric shock. Michael continued to hold out the bowl long after that contact was broken, trying to understand what had just happened.

When he placed the chili on the table in front of him, he was grateful for the excuse it gave to lower his head. As he did, he tried to reconstruct what he had seen in the kid's eyes.

Maybe it had been the directness of that stare, or the surprise of the color against the wind-burned skin. He felt as if some unspoken connection had been made. Or at least attempted.

"McAdams here's the new man," Quarrels said, speaking around a mouthful. "Starts tomorrow. Beaumont, you show him what to do."

Only Mapes looked up. The others continued to shovel chili into their mouths. Michael wondered which of them was Beaumont, and how much help he could expect with the blood samples they were going to be taking.

Across the table, Sal Johnson pushed back his chair. He picked up his empty bowl and utensils and carried them toward the kitchen. He didn't return with seconds as Michael had anticipated. Instead, after he'd deposited his dishes, he crossed the dining hall to disappear down the hall.

The ritual was repeated, as one by one the men returned their dishes to the kitchen and left. The kid was maybe the third or fourth to depart. Eventually only Charlie Quarrels and Ralph Mapes remained.

"I do something wrong?" Michael asked.

Mapes looked up to grin at him even as he scraped the last bite of chili out of his bowl.

It was Quarrels who answered. "They ain't big talkers."

"Glad to know it wasn't me."

''You need any help tomorrow, you ask. Nate's the best with the needle. He'll show you what to do.''

''Nate?''

''Nate Beaumont. The one sitting beside you.''

''The kid?''

''Says he's twenty,'' Mapes said. ''Believe that and I got me a bridge I wanna talk to you about.''

''Runaway?''

''I ain't never asked him,'' the foreman said. The tone was obviously intended to discourage further discussion of the subject.

Across the table Mapes raised his brows, looking directly at Michael. A warning, or an expression of sympathy?

''Breakfast at six. We start in to work at six-thirty.'' Quarrels pushed back his chair, almost drowning out the last of those instructions.

Mapes got up, too, trailing him across to the kitchen and then out through the door to the hall. Neither spoke to Michael again.

Left behind in the empty dining room, he put his spoon down, giving up all pretense of eating. He had been immersed in dozens of alien cultures during his years of service, first in the military and then with the agency. This one would rival any of them for strangeness.

He had known taciturn men before, but these barely acknowledged one another's existence. If this was the extent of their social interaction, it was no wonder the turnover was high.

He couldn't blame anyone who chose to leave this place. He'd been here less than four hours and he was already aware that the atmosphere was decidedly strange. And that business about the ranch being a research facility was just odd enough to make him decide that even if what was going on here had nothing to do with the Langworthy kidnapping, it was something he intended to understand before he left.

Young Nate Beaumont seemed the ideal place to start.

Chapter Four

It was not yet noon, and Michael already knew a lot about the kid he'd been assigned to partner with. Due to his years on the Royal Flush, he had worked with a lot of ranch hands. There were those who grew to hate the creatures they tended, their small cruelties deliberate. More common were the ones who no longer saw the animals as anything other than commodities, the reason they had a job. Something to protect because that's what they were paid to do.

Working in the morning's dusty confusion of sheep and dogs, it would have been easy to pick up on those attitudes. Nate Beaumont manifested neither. He was quick and efficient in taking the blood samples, but he was also careful not to unduly frighten or hurt any of the ewes or lambs they handled.

What they were doing was hot, backbreaking work. Michael had discarded his denim jacket by ten o'clock. The kid was still wearing his long-sleeved shirt, a near twin to the one he'd worn yesterday. Beneath it was a waffle-weave thermal underwear top, its three-button neckline visible at the open throat of the plaid. And despite the growing intensity of the sun, he showed no inclination to shed his outer garment as most of the other men had already done.

"What do they do with them?" Michael asked.

The kid didn't raise his head, slipping the needle into the vein in the ewe's neck, which he'd expertly located beneath the close-crimped fleece.

"The blood samples, I mean," Michael prodded.

"Don't know."

"You never asked?"

The answer was a negative motion that set the bowl-cut brown hair swinging. Nate withdrew the needle, and Michael reached for the yellow plastic tag on the sheep's ear.

He was holding her around the head, as the shearers did. She didn't seem to even realize she'd been stuck.

"Because you don't give a damn?"

"Because it's none of my business."

There had been no direct eye contact between them as there had at dinner last night. It hadn't been necessary. The routine they'd worked out, virtually without discussion, ran like clockwork.

Michael dragged the sheep to the table, where Beaumont drew the blood. When that was done, Michael read aloud the number from the animal's tag, and the kid wrote it on an adhesive label, which he then pressed around the vial. He had rarely looked up in the long hours they'd worked together.

"And you aren't even curious?" Michael prodded.

"No."

It had been like this all morning. Nate spoke only when asked a direct question and then in the fewest possible words, his voice so low Michael strained to catch the words above the constant noise of the pens.

"You're supposed to be teaching *him* how to do that," Charlie Quarrels yelled from outside the fence. "You two change places."

Michael glanced up to find the foreman leaning on the top rail, watching them. Nate didn't look at Quarrels, but he laid the syringe, which he'd already made ready, back on the table. Without a word, he walked around to where Michael was holding one of the spring lambs.

A small, straw-colored female, she was anxiously watching as her mother was being forced through the exit shoot by Sal Johnson. The lamb voiced her displeasure at that maternal desertion loud and clear.

The adult sheep seemed accustomed to the procedure, but the lambs were a different story. That was part of the reason Michael dreaded having to use this one as a guinea pig for his untested methodology. Conscious that Quarrels was still watching, Michael gave the lamb over to Nate's more than competent hands and walked around to the front of the table.

He picked up the needle, and as the boy held the lamb in position, he bent over it, searching for the vein in its neck, as he'd watched Nate do a hundred times. The problem was it was less visible on the lambs than on the adults.

He did the best he could, sliding the needle in under the skin. Thankfully, the syringe began to fill with blood. The lamb bleated soulfully, but that seemed more a result of loneliness than pain.

When the vial was full, Michael slid the needle out and straightened. He had begun to turn toward the table to complete the procedure by labeling the vial. Nate's head was still bent, his left hand holding the small, curly lamb while his right found the tag.

A glitter of silver-gilt where the boy's lank hair fell forward at the crown caught Michael's eye. Obviously new growth, it was less than an eighth of an inch long. That line of demarcation between the pale, champagne-blond at the scalp and the muddy brown color of the rest of his hair could only be seen from this angle.

Nate called out the number and then released the lamb,

sending her scampering after her mother. Michael pretended to be occupied with the labeling as he considered the implications of what he'd just seen.

It wouldn't be all that unusual for a boy this age to dye his hair. The more likely scenario, however, would be to go in the other direction. To change the color from a dull brown to that shimmering blond.

The more he thought about it, the more he realized that the opposite transformation made no sense, *unless* what he'd suspected last night was true. The kid was on the run.

And for some reason, the mystery of who Nate Beaumont might be hiding from and, more importantly, why was far more intriguing than what would become of the hundreds of vials they had filled this morning with sheep's blood.

"EVERY ANIMAL in the herd is sampled," Michael said into his satellite phone. "They bring a part of the flock down from the high pasture on a rotating basis, draw blood and then return them."

"And no one knows what's done with the samples that are collected?" Colleen asked.

"If they do, they aren't saying," Michael said. "Given the lack of communication among the hands, that's not surprising. I've never seen a stranger conglomeration. Could you run some prints if I sent them to you?"

"We have access to the national database. You have some reason—"

"Just covering the bases." It was probably a long shot, especially where the kid was concerned, but worth a try. "Before we get into fingerprints, how about running a name for me. See what you come up with."

He heard a rustle of paper on her end, thankful for the clarity of the sophisticated satellite phone's transmission. It was the same one he'd used during his last year with the agency. He had taped the phone inside the heater when he'd left to go down to the cabin for breakfast this morning. As far as he could tell, it hadn't been discovered. Actually, he had found no evidence that anyone had been inside the trailer during his absence, something he hadn't taken for granted.

It would be a pain remembering to take the phone out of its hiding place and charge it during the few hours the generator ran in the evenings, but it was a necessity. This was the only way he had of communicating with the outside world. And the longer he was here, the more detached he felt from it.

"Okay, shoot," Colleen said.

"Nate Beaumont," he said, spelling the last name. "Since that's probably not his real name, consider anything close. Same initials, for example. I doubt you'll find anything criminal. I'd be more interested in missing persons. Lost or abducted kids. Runaways. Maybe sixteen or seventeen. Blue-eyed blonde. Five-ten or -eleven."

"You think he's involved in something on the ranch?"

"I think he's hiding out here. I'm curious to know why."

"Okay," she said again, but he could hear skepticism in her voice.

He didn't blame her. Even he couldn't put his finger on what bothered him about the kid. It was like having someone's name on the tip of your tongue and still not being able to figure out who they were.

"Everything all right there?" she asked, the note of sisterly anxiety clear, even across the distance.

"Meaning am I all right?"

There was a beat of silence. "Are you?"

"I smell like sheep. A lot of sheep. Other than that I

can't complain. You *did* intend for this to be boring, didn't you?''

Another pause.

''Is it?'' At least her voice had lightened, losing that tinge of concern he hated.

''I'll let you know after I've been here a few more days. By the way, don't call me even if you find something on the kid. Let me make the contact. It's probably safer.''

Without giving her time to respond, he punched the off button with his thumb then laid the phone on the floor beside the bunk. He swung his bare legs up onto the mattress, grimacing as the left one protested. He leaned back against the limp pillow, his hands behind his head, fingers interlocked as he waited for the pain pills he'd taken after his shower to kick in.

There was nothing unusual about a ranch participating in research. Sometimes the money from a study was all that kept a small operation afloat.

Most ranches operated on a pretty narrow profit margin. Judging by the shoddy accommodations and the quality of the four meals he'd been served so far, this was one of them.

He couldn't see how a run-down sheep operation could have any connection with the Langworthy kidnapping, despite Senator Gettys having a share in the place and the strange atmosphere. And frankly, he was too exhausted to do any serious thinking about the question tonight. At least tomorrow wouldn't be as hard physically.

He and Beaumont had been instructed to move the sheep they'd taken samples from today back up to higher pastures. It had been a while since he'd straddled a horse, but it wasn't the kind of thing you forgot. Thankfully it would involve the use of a different set of muscles from those that ached so badly now despite the long, semi-hot shower he'd just taken.

Maybe away from the others, Nate would be more forthcoming. If there *were* something shady going on here, he'd stake his reputation the kid wasn't involved in it.

And if he were wrong, then by trying to pick Nate's brain about what he had seen during the months he'd worked here, Michael would be staking a whole lot more than that.

NICOLA CARSON leaned forward, letting the weak, tepid stream of water run over the back of her neck and bowed head. There wasn't much she wouldn't give to be able to take a really good shower. The kind she used to take for granted. Strong spray. Gallons of hot water. Lots of steam.

Actually, there *was* something she wouldn't give. Which was why she was living here on the Half Spur in the first place.

Living. Despite the primitive conditions and the fact that she hadn't seen her mother in more than eight months, she wasn't ready to risk her life in order to leave.

Most of the time she'd felt safe here. The exception to that feeling of security was when someone new entered the picture. Someone like McAdams.

She reminded herself that she had had this same sense of impending doom every time a hand signed on. It had gradually faded as each was assimilated into the strange world in which she now existed.

Of course, none of the others had seemed as interested in that world as Mac did. His questions today had made her increasingly uncomfortable.

He was different from the drifters and misfits Quarrels normally hired. She had decided early on those choices were deliberate, which made his hiring of McAdams even more peculiar.

She turned, letting the water run down between her breasts. Unconsciously, she cupped her palms under them, turning from side to side to let the spray wash play over her chest.

It was only at times like these, in the privacy of the tiny shower inside her trailer, that she could afford to acknowledge her femininity. The rest of the day she tried to merge totally into the role she was playing. A role that had so far kept her alive.

That was the other thing that bothered her about Mc-Adams. The way he made her feel. Like a woman—and that was something she couldn't afford.

Maybe it was because he was undeniably attractive. Exactly the kind of man she had always been drawn to.

Or maybe, after months of being virtually ignored by everyone around her, it was the way he looked at her. Really looked. As if he were trying to see through her.

She opened her eyes at the thought, staring at the plastic laminate in front of her as the words echoed in her brain.

As if he were trying to see through her.

That's exactly what he did. He watched her. He questioned her. He studied her. As if he were trying to figure out who and what she was.

Hand trembling, she reached out and shut off the flow of water. She forced her eyes to focus on her fingers, which were still gripping the knob. Assessing them.

Short, broken nails. Sunburned skin that always looked a little grimy. A few half-healed nicks and scrapes.

There was absolutely nothing feminine about them. Nothing to give her away.

And she had always had a deep voice for a woman. Everyone commented on it. A whiskey voice, her grandmother had called it. That huskiness was one of the things that had made her think she might be able to pull this off.

And in the six months she'd lived here, no one had seemed to think twice about its timbre.

Her size, too, was in her favor. She was tall and thin enough to appear boyish, especially in the kind of shapeless garments she wore.

She hadn't been able to do anything to disguise her features, other than keep her head down. She had done that today, her gaze focused on the task at hand. Last night, however...

Looking at him had been a mistake. She'd known it as soon as their eyes had made contact, but by then it had been too late to do anything about it.

Too late. Too late.

She doubled up her fists and slammed them against the wall of the shower. Closing her eyes, she leaned forward, laying her forehead against her clenched hands.

After several frozen seconds, she opened them, stretching her fingers flat against the stall. Then she pushed away from it, standing straight and tall. Fighting for control.

That kind of thinking was nothing but sheer, mindless paranoia. McAdams was a new hand. That's all he was. There had been a dozen before him, and when he was gone, a dozen others would follow.

She couldn't allow herself to become suspicious. That wariness would make her self-conscious. Inclined to say or do something stupid when he was around. She needed to go on acting exactly as she had been before he'd shown up here.

Just another drifter, she told herself, determined not to let that smothering sense of terror that had followed the attack at the Metro station take control of her again. He's just a man. Just like all the others on the ranch.

Except he wasn't.

The image of strange, blue-green eyes that seemed to see

through her was suddenly in her head. Hands that moved with a completely masculine grace. Corded forearms, tanned and covered with a fuzz of gold. Far lighter than the hair that curled against the collar of his shirt. Maybe that was just a trick of the sunlight—

A trick of the sunlight.

The thought was terrifying. She reached out and grabbed the frayed, graying towel off the bar. She wrapped it around her body, sarong-style, and stepped hurriedly out of the enclosure.

The mirror over the sink was clouded with age and moisture. Almost afraid of what she might see in it, she fumbled for the hand towel on the rack and after a second's hesitation, used it to wipe off the surface.

Then she leaned closer, lifting her bangs with her right hand. Along the scalp was a narrow line of blond. She couldn't remember the last time she'd put the dye on, but obviously it had been too long ago.

She dropped the bangs, parting the hair on the top of her head with shaking fingers. Turning to catch the light from the bare bulb above the sink. Even in this dimness, the new growth was clearly visible, several shades lighter than the rest.

And she must have ducked her head a hundred times today. Hiding her face. Concealing, or so she thought, the one thing that might give her away. The one thing that might make him question. Wonder. Think about her at all.

And tomorrow she would be alone with him all day. Away from the safety of the pens and the public areas and other people. She could feel that mindless apprehension growing, tightening her chest and making it hard to breathe.

Drifter. He's just a drifter. She fought against her panic, repeating the words like a litany. Determined to force their reality into her brain. *He isn't here because of you. You are no more to him than Quarrels or any of the others.*

Long into the night, eyes open and staring in the darkness, she made herself say them over and over, trying desperately to believe that they might be true.

Chapter Five

They were halfway back to the ranch when Michael pulled up his gelding. He dismounted and then stooped, despite the protesting muscles in his back and thighs, to run his hands gently over the horse's left front fetlock. The two border collies that had come with them trotted over, ears pricked, and stood near him.

"Something wrong?"

Nate Beaumont had reined in a little farther back on the trail, behind Michael. Eyes narrowed, he watched Michael from under the wide brim of a battered straw hat.

"Seems a little lame." As he offered the explanation, Michael lifted the gelding's foot, pretending to examine the frog. "Got a pick?" he asked without looking up.

After a slight hesitation, Nate urged the mare forward, bringing her alongside the gelding. Michael put out his hand, palm upward, to receive the equestrian knife he was offered. As he unfolded the hoof pick from the multi-bladed instrument, he slanted a sideways look at the boy.

"Picked up a stone?" Nate asked.

"I don't think it's been there long enough to do any damage. He's only been favoring it a minute or two."

He bent over the gelding's foot, his body shielding it from the boy's view, and pretended to pry out the nonexistent obstruction. After a moment, he dropped the leg then ran a soothing hand over his mount's neck. He turned to face Nate, folding the pick back into the knife before he held it up to him.

"I need to get one of these. You never know when a knife might come in handy. Especially out here."

For a long moment Beaumont didn't move. In contrast to their customary avoidance, the sapphire eyes locked on Michael's face. He would have sworn that what he saw in them was raw fear.

"Your knife," he prodded, moving it up and down to draw Nate's attention. "Thanks for the loan."

The boy swallowed, the movement strong enough to be visible down the column of his throat before it disappeared into the high collar of the thermal undershirt he wore. Michael's eyes had followed the motion, and he felt again that nagging sensation that there was something important about what he'd just seen. Something he was missing and shouldn't be.

Before he could figure it out, Nate's hand closed over the knife, removing it from his grasp. "You probably should at that. They're useful for all kinds of things."

Maybe he thought it was strange Michael didn't have a knife. After all, most cowboys carried them. He had when he'd worked on the Royal Flush.

His equipment requirements in the days since then had been very different. He *had* considered bringing the Glock up here, but the thought of acquiring a folding knife had never crossed his mind.

"How about a breather?" he suggested. "Give him a chance to figure out he's not crippled." Because he could see the resolution to refuse building in the kid's eyes, he added, "I could stand one, too. Stretch my leg."

Nate had never mentioned his limp. No one but Quarrels

had commented on it. And although the knee had been stiff and painful this morning from the stooping he'd done yesterday, it hadn't kept him from climbing on board the gelding. There was no way he would have let it, no matter how sore it had been.

Today's assignment, however, hadn't quite worked out as Michael had hoped. There had been no opportunity to ask Beaumont any questions. And maybe that had been deliberate on Nate's part.

Going up to the high pasture, they had ridden on opposite sides of the flock, letting the Half Spur's collies do the actual herding. During the ride back down, Nate had kept his distance, hanging behind Michael on the trail, letting the dogs run between.

That's why Michael had come up with the story about the gelding's lameness. And now he needed a reason to prolong this brief time alone with the boy. As he'd expected, the veiled reference to his disability worked like a charm.

Nate eased down off the mare, saddle creaking in the stillness of the mountain air. Once Michael saw he'd succeeded in getting Nate to dismount, he pretended to ignore the kid. He walked the gelding slowly around the small clearing as if assessing the injury, the dogs following behind him. As part of the act, he didn't bother to try to hide his own aching muscles.

When he'd completed the circle and was returning to the starting point, he realized Nate had been watching the performance. Watching him, rather than the horse.

"You smoke?" he asked.

A lot of kids that age did, and it would provide another reason to prolong the break. Nate shook his head, his gaze now pointedly considering the trail down to the compound.

"Something bothering you?"

The kid turned, his eyes widened slightly. "What does that mean?"

"I'm just curious why you're so damn skittish."

"Skittish?"

"You keep to yourself. You keep your head down. You don't talk. In my experience that means a man's afraid of something or he's hiding something. I just wondered which it was in your case."

"I don't know what you're talking about."

"I'm talking about finding a good place to hide and then laying low. Trying to keep yourself off somebody's radar screen," Michael said, realizing that he had unconsciously repeated Colleen's words about him. "I've done that a few times in my life."

Nate shook his head. "I like working here. I like the country. The isolation."

"So your family knows where you are."

"I don't have family. Not everybody does."

"No family. No friends. No past."

And no denial. The regard from those blue eyes was steady. Whatever fear Michael thought he'd seen in them before had been conquered or controlled.

"You about ready to head out?" the kid asked. "If we're not back by six, there won't be anything to eat until breakfast tomorrow."

Since it was midafternoon, his excuse for leaving wasn't terribly convincing. Given a chance to be on their own and without supervision, most cowboys would find a way to keep from going back before suppertime. It was almost expected.

"What's the rush? Quarrels will just find something else for us to do. Relax."

Nate's lips flattened, but he didn't argue. He led the mare over to an outcropping of rock and sat down. His mount began nibbling at the few patches of rough grass growing nearby. He signaled to the dogs and they lay down in a shady spot.

Michael made a pretense of walking the gelding for a few more minutes before he limped over to join Nate. Instead of sitting down beside him and taking a chance of scaring the kid off, he put his left foot up on the rock, resting his weight on his sound right leg. The position relieved some of the stress on the damaged knee.

"So how long you been here?"

"About six months." The kid was ostensibly watching the two horses, which had begun ranging farther afield in search of more promising grazing.

"And the others? How long for them?"

"Less." The admission was reluctantly made. "Nobody stays long."

"Except you."

"I told you. I like it here."

Despite the determined front the kid was putting up, Michael's conviction that he was on the run was still strong. There wasn't much point in trying to push past this kind of stonewalling, however.

Maybe after he'd been here a while and earned Nate's trust, the boy would be willing to confide in him. Until then, all he could do was keep an eye on Beaumont and at the same time do the job he'd been sent here for. Maybe if he couldn't get Nate to talk about himself, he could get him to talk about the Half Spur.

"You like this place despite the weirdness?"

Nate turned his head, looking directly at him. His eyes were carefully blank.

"Those blood samples, for example," Michael went on. "Nobody knows what they're for or where they're sent. You don't think that's weird? And Quarrels? Don't tell me you don't think there's plenty strange about him." No answer. By this time, of course, he wasn't expecting one. "It makes me wonder what's *really* going on here. And since you've been here a while…"

He let the sentence trail encouragingly. There was no response.

"Suit yourself," he said after the silence stretched long and empty.

He pushed off the rock he'd been propped against, intending to admit defeat by going to round up the horses. As he put his left foot on the ground, the damaged knee buckled unexpectedly, throwing him off balance. He put out his hand, grabbing for something solid to keep from falling.

His reaching fingers encountered Nate Beaumont's shoulder, closing over it like a lifeline. With its support, he managed to right himself. As soon as he had, he loosened his grip on the kid.

Nate jumped to his feet, assuming a fighter's crouch directly in front of him. In his right hand he held the equestrian knife he'd lent Michael minutes before, its short blade exposed.

Given the speed with which it had appeared, Michael realized belatedly that the boy must have already had the knife out. His hand had rested on the rock near his leg, the blade obviously hidden alongside it. Open and ready.

Michael straightened, leaning away from the weapon. He held up his hands, shoulder high, their palms toward the kid in a classically submissive posture.

"Whoa," he said softly. "Take it easy."

The boy's eyes were feral, his entire body tensed and waiting. "Stay the hell away from me," he said, his voice as menacing as the knife he held.

"Look, whatever you're thinking—"

Michael had made the mistake of lowering his hands as he talked. The knife moved, threatening his gut.

"What I *think* is that you ask too many questions."

"I thought I could help," Michael said, his tone quiet and reasoned.

"I don't need your help. *Or* your concern."

"Okay. Whatever you say. Just put the knife down."

"So we can *talk?*"

The tone of that mocking question was cynical and distrustful. And more bitter than the situation seemed to warrant.

Maybe he *had* pushed too hard, Michael acknowledged, but pulling a knife seemed an overreaction that needed some explanation.

"We don't have to talk. Not if you don't want to."

"How'd you find me?"

Confused, Michael shook his head, keeping his eyes on the blade. "I don't know what you're talking about."

"I'm talking about how *handy* you thought a knife would be. How you ought to get one."

Again Michael shook his head. "You've lost me. First of all, I didn't *find* you, because I wasn't looking for you. And what I said about the knife? That was just making conversation. It didn't mean a thing."

Nate laughed, the sound abrupt, lacking any hint of amusement. The blade didn't waver. Although he was holding the knife properly—blade up, handle down—there was something about his stance that spoke of desperation rather than intimidation.

"Just like before, I guess."

"Kid, I don't know what happened to you, or who did what, but I didn't come here looking for you. I've never had any contact with you before yesterday."

For the first time, doubt touched the determination in the

boy's face. A doubt he quickly denied. His features hardened again.

"You're a liar. You've been at me since you got here."

"Because I thought you might know something about what's going on up here."

"Like what?" The confusion seemed genuine.

"The blood samples for one. The people who drift in and out."

"Why do *you* care about any of that?"

Michael weighed how much he could say. He needed to win the boy's trust, if for no other reason than to keep him from sticking a knife in his back the next time he decided Michael should be the target of his paranoid fantasy.

Paranoid. Maybe the kid *was* crazy. After all, it wasn't exactly normal to react to a few unwanted questions by pulling a knife.

As much as he'd like to know what Nate Beaumont had observed in the months he'd lived here, when you were working undercover you had to pick your snitches as carefully as your allies. He wasn't sure the boy could ever become either.

Neither could he be allowed to continue to pose a threat. The kid looked like some wild animal, cornered and defending itself because that's all it had ever known. Fighting for survival. And the only way you ever tamed a wild animal…

Broken-down has-been or not, if he couldn't put some fear—if not some respect—in those hostile baby-blues, he needed to call Colleen and tell her to get one of her hotshots up here to check this place out. And it would be a cold day in Hell before he'd be willing to do that.

"Look," he said persuasively, taking the critical step forward.

The boy lost his chance when he didn't use the knife as

soon as Michael moved. By the time Nate realized what was happening, Michael had already grasped the wrist of his right hand, the one with the blade. He jerked it upward, having more success than he'd expected because the boy was clearly surprised by the move.

At the same time Michael gritted his teeth, dreading the agony he knew would result, and put all his weight on his damaged leg. He used the sound one to sweep the boy's feet out from under him.

They fell together, Michael on top. He held onto the boy's wrist, which was now stretched above his head, in order to control the knife.

For a moment he could do nothing but lie there speechless, stunned by the bolt of lightning that had seared through his knee as they'd gone down. It didn't matter. The breath had gone out of Nate's lungs in a satisfying whoosh, leaving him openmouthed and gasping on the ground, Michael's body spread on top of his.

The kid was nowhere near as solidly built as those layers of clothing seemed to indicate. Now, his body pressed closely along the entire length of Michael's, Nate seemed much thinner. More fragile. More—

Sensations bombarded Michael's brain in rapid-fire sequence as the pain in his knee faded to a level that would allow him to think. The last thought that registered on his consciousness was immediately rejected as impossible.

And then, all those small, telltale anomalies he hadn't been able to put together fell into place in one fell swoop. His fingers still gripping the wrist of the hand that held the knife, Michael pushed himself away from the torso of the slender body beneath him to look down into dark blue eyes and the too-delicate features that surrounded them.

"What the hell—?" he breathed.

Although the woman who lay beneath him, firmly pinned

to the ground by his weight, was no longer fighting to pull air into her lungs, she didn't bother to answer. She continued to look up into his eyes, her own filled with fear and despair.

Then, even as he watched, too shocked by his discovery to think of anything else to say, they slowly began to glaze with tears.

Chapter Six

Damn it. Damn *him,* Nicki raged inwardly as she struggled not to cry.

With what appeared to be very little effort, the man who called himself McAdams had thrown her to the ground, at the same time totally negating the threat of the knife. She had been armed and he hadn't, and he had still gotten the best of her.

All these months, she had thought about what she would do if she were again confronted by her attacker. She had foolishly imagined she was prepared for that eventuality. Determined and desperate enough to kill in order to protect herself.

McAdams, however, had moved so quickly that she'd had no time to react. His fingers had fastened around her wrist, and she'd been flat on her back almost before she'd realized what he'd done.

Yet she had been prepared for something like that to happen from the time he'd dismounted. Prepared, but obviously not ready, she admitted bitterly. And now he was going to kill her, just as he had tried to do before.

"Who are you?" he demanded.

She turned her head to the side, closing her eyes. Refusing to look into his. It was over. She had failed, and she knew she was about to pay the price for that failure.

She wasn't going to watch while he did it. And she certainly wasn't going to respond to his questions.

"Answer me, damn it. Since you obviously *aren't* Nate Beaumont, who the hell are you?"

It was only with the second repetition of the question that she recognized its significance. If he didn't know who she was, then he hadn't tracked her here. He couldn't be the man who had attacked her in Washington. A man whose arrival she had been dreading since she'd chosen this—of all places—to hide.

Almost unwillingly, she turned her head so that they were again face-to-face, the weight of his body heavy on hers. To see her face, he had lifted his torso so that the hard wall of his chest no longer crushed her breasts. Along the rest of their length, they were still pressed together intimately. As if they were lovers.

Bizarrely, she found that intimacy neither terrified nor repelled her, maybe because of the insight she'd just had. Whatever the reason, she was no longer afraid of the man who pinned her to the ground. Although she was very much aware of him. *No longer as an enemy, but as a man.*

Something of what she was thinking must have been reflected in her eyes. Looking into them, his began to change, their dark pupils expanding outward into the rim of color.

That wasn't the only change she was aware of. Despite the fact that they were adversaries, despite the dangerous scenario that had put them into this position, through the thin fabric of the jeans he wore she felt the first stirrings of his erection.

"Answer me," he demanded again, choosing to ignore what was happening to his body. "I asked who you are."

Nicki closed her lips, swallowing against a new fear. Maybe this wasn't the man who had tried to kill her, but if the senator learned she was here, she opened herself up to the possibility that that man *would* find her. Or that Gettys would send someone else. Mutely, she shook her head.

"I'm not going to hurt you," McAdams said. His voice had softened persuasively. "I might even be able to help."

For someone who had been alone so long, there was an undeniable emotional pull to that promise, even if she couldn't afford to believe it. She had made it this far by keeping her mouth shut. Besides, why would someone be willing to accept any part of the risks she faced by helping her?

"How?"

She listened to her own question with a sense of disbelief. She hadn't intended to answer. She had intended to stay silent, no matter what he said. Somehow, the thought of having assistance, even from a stranger, had been too tempting not to respond to.

Her heart seemed to stop, every fiber of her being waiting for his answer. It took him so long to give it that the fragile hope his offer had engendered began to die.

"I have friends in high places."

She'd been warned by the self-mocking tone even before she saw the small, upward lift at the corners of his mouth. A very attractive mouth.

She couldn't remember the last time someone had smiled at her. That ridiculous burn of tears stung at the back of her eyes again.

"They better be in some pretty damned high ones," she said, relieved there was no hint in her voice of the ongoing urge to cry.

It took him maybe a second to figure that out. "Whoever you're afraid of is influential as well."

After another moment of internal debate over the wisdom of telling him even that much, she nodded. She was finding it very difficult to trust him with her secret. To let someone else into this world of deception she had constructed to hide in. Once she did, she knew there could be no turning back.

''Drop the knife, and I'll let you up,'' he offered as she tried to think.

Instead, her fingers tightened over its handle reflexively. To let go of the knife required yet another dimension of trust. Another step out of the shadows, and she still hadn't decided why she'd made the first.

Maybe because she'd reached the end of her own resources. She'd been here for months, and she was no closer to knowing what had set off that attempt on her life back in D.C. than when she'd arrived.

She still believed that this isolated ranch held the key to why someone wanted her dead. She just hadn't yet found the answer that she'd hoped would set her free. By now she had begun to fear she never would.

McAdams was interested in whatever was going on here. His questions, although discreet, had made that obvious to her from the first. Was it possible that someone else, perhaps those friends he'd mentioned, was also interested in Gettys and the Half Spur? If so, this man might represent the only chance she'd ever have to get her life back.

She forced her fingers to unfold from around the handle of the knife, an act of will. The hilt lay exposed on her outstretched palm as her eyes held his. He lifted her wrist off the ground and shook it, causing the blade to fall away. She didn't turn her head to watch, but she heard the small thump as it hit the dirt.

He moved then, releasing her hands and putting his right knee and palm on the ground. He pushed his upper body erect until he was on his knees, straddling her.

Without the warmth of his body over hers, she felt naked. Exposed. More vulnerable somehow than she had been while he'd held her prisoner.

He struggled to his feet. The process was not only awkward, but painful as well, judging by the small grunt of discomfort as he put weight on his left leg. McAdams might be practicing his own deceptions, but whatever was wrong with his knee didn't seem to be a part of them.

The stumble that had thrown him off balance, causing him to grab her shoulder, had been genuine. And she had reacted to it as if it were the attack she'd been expecting since he'd made his comment about needing a knife.

As soon as he was standing, he leaned forward, holding out his hand. For some reason she was reluctant to take it.

She had been the recipient of numerous offers of hands-up throughout her formative years. She had accepted all of them with a deep sense of gratitude. Including the one from Franklin Gettys.

Her belief that Senator Gettys was involved in the attempt on her life had created a deep-seated mistrust that had become almost impossible to overcome. Maybe accepting McAdams's help would be the first step in that direction.

She put her fingers into his and allowed him to pull her to her feet. As soon as he had, he bent to pick up the knife. He folded the blade inward and then held it out to her, the gesture mocking her suspicions.

Maybe that was the intent, she thought cynically. He had already demonstrated his ability to disarm her, even when she had thought she was prepared to kill him.

Without a word, she took the knife, sliding it into the pocket of her jeans, which were loose-fitting enough to hide its shape. When she raised her head again, she found he was watching her.

"I'm Michael Wellesley," he said, sticking out his right hand.

She didn't take it. Nor did she reciprocate with her own name. She was still struggling with the notion of giving up the information that she had protected so long.

"Are you FBI?" she asked.

"What makes you think the FBI would be interested in the Half Spur?"

She recognized the question as another attempt to find out what she knew without giving anything away himself.

"You said you have friends in high places."

"Not *those* places."

"But you are…" She hesitated, uncertain what she needed to hear him say.

"On the side of the angels?" he responded, his lips tilting again.

She wasn't sure this time if he was mocking himself or her. She hadn't been sure of that before, and yet she had trusted him enough to reveal that her enemies were also well placed. How much could she trust him now?

"I think I need more specific information than that."

But it was a start, she admitted. FBI or not, she really needed him to be one of the good guys.

"Michael Wellesley," he said again. "Formerly with military intelligence and the CIA."

The *CIA?* There was no way she could fit the agency in the framework of any scenario she'd imagined during the past eight months. For one thing, she thought they only worked internationally. Of course, he had qualified the information as "formerly."

"And currently?"

"For this to work, it's going to require some mutual sharing of information. I've told you my name. I think it's time for you to reciprocate."

"How do I know that's really your name?"

"If you're looking for identification," he said, letting his amusement show again, "that would be the last thing I'd have on me during an assignment."

"Then…you *are* on assignment?"

"I'm not here voluntarily. The accommodations alone should convince you of that."

Everything about him screamed something other than a drifter. It had from the first, which was the reason she'd been so wary. And he hadn't killed her when he had the chance. Not even when she had given him cause by pulling a knife on him.

Besides, the man in D.C. hadn't been interested in what she knew. All he'd wanted was to cut her throat.

"Nicki Carson," she said. "Nicola, actually."

She expected her name to mean something to him. It was obvious that it didn't.

"That's a start," he said. "Keep going."

"I was an intern for Senator Gettys."

"Franklin Gettys."

The inflection hadn't really been questioning, but she nodded. "I had worked for him for almost a year when…"

She let the explanation trail. She had never resolved her own doubts about what had happened. Now that she was being asked to explain what had sent her into hiding, her suspicions seemed almost too flimsy to share. They were also completely unsubstantiated, despite her attempts to investigate the Half Spur.

"Go on," Wellesley urged.

She shook her head, the movement slow. Unconscious. "It sounds unbelievable. I know that. I just can't come up with anything else that would explain what happened."

"Why don't you tell me what you think without trying to justify *why* you think it?"

Accepting his reasoning, she nodded and plunged on. "I think I saw something I wasn't supposed to see. A tax document that pertained to the senator's ownership of the Half Spur. He was out in the hallway when the fax came through. I thought it was important, so I took it to him." She mentally reconstructed the events as she talked, reliving them as she had a hundred times. "I don't know. Maybe I should have waited. Maybe that's what upset him, rather than what the fax contained."

"And what was that?"

She took a calming breath, trying to frame what she needed to say into a rational argument. It was hard, because she had never been able to convince herself that what she'd seen that day could possibly be important enough to make the senator want her dead. She had finally arrived at this explanation because she couldn't think of anything else that important either.

"I didn't read it. Not the whole thing. I realized pretty quickly that it had to do with Senator Gettys and some property. Nothing involving the campaign or politics."

"And the part you *did* read?"

"My impression was that it was just a quarterly report on the ranch. Probably for tax purposes, like I said. Nothing incriminating."

"You're sure it was this ranch?"

She nodded. "It was named in the document. When I brought it to him, he was…furious. There's no other word for it. I'd never seen him like that, so it made his reaction more frightening. He grabbed the fax out of my hand and starting yelling at me. I still didn't understand what I'd done wrong. It was more a personal attack than a correction of office protocol. And he'd never spoken to me like that before."

She didn't mention the other thing that made the whole

episode even more shocking—the senator's previous kid-glove treatment of her. When she had first started working for him, his manner had verged on flirtatious, especially for a man who was a relative newlywed. She'd tried to put it down to an old-fashioned idea about how men should treat women—some kind of misplaced gallantry.

Long before the night of his blowup, however, Gettys's manner had become suggestive enough to make her consider leaving, despite the fact that being an intern for the senator had represented a dream. One of the many that night had shattered.

"And then?"

The hard part. The part that would make her sound paranoid. Like some idiot who would let an attempted mugging send her into a tailspin.

That was something else she'd tried to rationalize. Why she was so sure that man had been trying to kill her. There was no definitive answer. Nothing except her absolute certainty that he had been.

"Someone began following me."

Unconsciously, as she'd considered how to tell him this, she had allowed her eyes to fall. Now she forced them up, focusing on Michael Wellesley's face. Because she could detect no trace of disbelief or amusement in his features, she made herself continue.

"Sometimes it was nothing more than a feeling. A chill on the back of my neck. A dozen times I made up my mind that it was all in my head, but I knew he was there. It got to the point where I thought I could tell when he was behind me."

She searched his eyes, again looking for ridicule. There was nothing there but a patient waiting.

"About three weeks after the fax came through, the senator asked me to take a disk over to campaign headquarters.

It was already late, and the reelection office was halfway across town. I wondered why he didn't just let me courier it over the next day, but I didn't feel I could afford to refuse. He'd been distant since the incident with the fax, so I thought he was looking for an excuse to let me go. If I left, I wanted it to be on my terms. Not because he'd fired me.''

She was talking too much. She'd thought so much about what had happened that every detail was burned on her consciousness. Part of that had been an effort to understand the event, but mostly it had been an attempt to make sure she was right about what the attack meant. It had changed her life in such a fundamental way that she couldn't afford to be wrong.

''He didn't offer to pay for a cab, so I took the Metro. As I entered that station, someone attacked me. It wasn't a robbery. He didn't grab my purse when I dropped it. I believe he had a knife, and he intended to kill me.''

''Because you saw a fax about this ranch?''

Michael Wellesley's inflection was carefully neutral, but she had asked that same question too many times not to understand its implications.

''I know how crazy that sounds, but…I can't think of anything else. Believe me, I've tried. Why would someone else want to kill me?''

''Why would Gettys?''

She didn't have an answer to that. She had never had one. That was the reason she'd come to the Half Spur. To try to understand why it had happened.

''It *had* to have something to do with this ranch,'' she repeated adamantly. ''Whatever you're thinking, I'm not making this up. And I'm not wrong about what that man was trying to do. My purse was lying on the ground and he ignored it.''

"Okay, not a robbery, but women are attacked every day. Maybe this was just a random—"

"There was nothing random about my being followed. And don't forget that it was Gettys who sent me there that night. That's how the attacker knew where I'd be."

"If he'd been following you, he'd know anyway," Michael said reasonably. "He wouldn't need Gettys to send you somewhere. Maybe this guy was a stalker, someone who saw you and fixated on you."

"He had adjusted the security camera somehow so it didn't point to the area where he attacked me. He *had* to have done that in advance. It couldn't have been spur of the moment. Someone had to have told him I'd be there, and only Gettys knew. He sent me there."

At least he didn't have an answer for that, she thought, feeling she had scored a point.

"How'd you get away?"

"I fought him off."

For the first time she read skepticism in his eyes. And why wouldn't he be skeptical of that claim, considering how easily he'd disarmed her?

"I guess he wasn't as good as you are," she said, not bothering to hide her resentment that he was questioning what she was telling him.

"I would think Senator Gettys could afford the best. Especially for something as potentially important as a murder for hire."

This was exactly why she had never gone to the police. You don't accuse one of the most powerful men in the Senate of attempted murder. Not without proof. And proof was something she'd never had.

"You think I'm making this up?"

"I think you have very little to tie Gettys to what happened."

"Don't you mean *if* it happened?"

"*Something* happened, or you wouldn't be here. I'm just doing what any good cop or prosecutor you tell this story to is going to do. I'm asking for something more solid than a coldness on the back of your neck to connect Gettys and the Half Spur to that attack in Washington."

She had nothing more solid. Nothing but her absolute conviction that, because there was nothing else, those things had to be connected. Apparently that wasn't enough for him.

"Then I guess you can't help me after all."

Angry that the hope he'd offered had been nothing but smoke and mirrors, she turned, intending to head for the grazing horses. Michael caught her arm before she could take the first step.

"Please, let me go," she ordered quietly.

She wouldn't try to fight him. He'd already demonstrated how ineffective her efforts would be. There was no need to make a fool of herself twice.

"Tell me about the Half Spur. You must have learned something in the months you've spent here."

"It's a sheep ranch," she said, mocking the question. Mocking him. "They shear the sheep and then they sell the wool."

"And they take blood samples."

"As part of a research project." Her tone was less grudging. This was something she'd considered when she'd first arrived, but there was no pretense of hiding the sampling, which argued there was nothing sinister about it.

"A project no one here knows anything about."

"Quarrels knows."

"Why do you say that?"

There was an edge of interest in his voice that hadn't been there when she'd told him her story. But then that's why he was here. Not because of what had happened to her, but because of whatever was going on at this ranch.

Which was why she'd come as well, she realized. Even if he didn't believe her story, maybe she could use him.

"Because he's the one who packs the samples for transport to wherever it is they end up."

"He mails them?"

She thought about it, wondering why she'd never considered that might be what he was doing.

"It's possible. I always thought he delivered them personally. He packs them into insulated containers. They aren't wrapped for mailing, but I guess he could take them to a packaging company in town. Have it done there."

"I'm not sure they'd be eager to handle something like that," Michael said. It sounded as if he were thinking out loud. "Handling biohazards requires a special license."

"Biohazards?"

"For all they could know."

He was right. No one would be willing to ship blood products about which they knew nothing. Besides, it was probably illegal.

"So wherever they go," she said, working her way to the conclusion he'd already reached, "you think he must take them himself."

"It seems likely. Now if we knew how long he's gone each time…" He tilted his head, waiting for her give him the information.

"He leaves at night. Late. Maybe eleven. He's always back for breakfast the next morning, and the truck is empty."

"Every week?"

"Every time we draw blood," she corrected, feeling like the star pupil. "Sometimes that's every two weeks. I'm not sure I understand why the length of time he's gone is important.''

"Because it gives us a starting point to figure out where he takes them.''

"Somewhere within a three and a half hour drive.''

She felt like a fool for not having put that information together before now. It was just that she'd decided early on that the blood samples weren't relevant to what had happened to her.

There was nothing secret about them. Quarrels had told her when he'd hired her that they were part of the job. He told everyone that.

She'd grown up on a farm. She was familiar with the government hoops her father had had to jump through. If he could have gotten paid to draw blood from his animals, there was no doubt in her mind that he would have had the whole family lined up to do it.

"We take a map and draw a circle with the compound in the center and a three and a half hour radius," Michael said. "It gives us somewhere to start.''

"That's a lot of territory.''

"Or we can follow him.''

We. The word resonated in her heart more strongly than it should have. She had been alone for so long that having someone on her side, even if he didn't believe her about the attack, made her throat ache.

"You knew more than you thought about this place.''

He had probably been counting on that. And on his own ability to ask the right questions. Still, the approval in his tone was balm to the sense of failure she'd lived with all these months.

Always an overachiever, she wasn't accustomed to failure. Besides, there was something about Michael Wellesley's confidence that was contagious. He'd been sent here to do a job, essentially the same one she'd been trying to do for months. The difference was he believed he'd succeed.

She believed he would, too, she recognized with a flicker of surprise. Whoever and whatever this man was, it was clear to her that he was accustomed to accomplishing whatever he set out to do.

She felt again that small, fragile flutter of hope with which she'd first responded to his offer of help. Who his friends were didn't matter. Just the thought of someone this determined being on her side was enough for now.

Chapter Seven

"Nicola Carson," Michael said into his satellite phone. "She says she was Gettys's intern."

"Of course. I knew I'd heard the name as soon as you said it, but I couldn't think where," Colleen said. "Nicki Carson. Are you saying *she's* your Nate Beaumont?"

"One in the same. She says she was attacked back in Washington. That someone tried to kill her because she saw a document pertaining to this ranch."

"She says that's why she disappeared?"

"You sound..." He didn't finish the sentence because he wasn't quite sure what he'd heard in his sister's voice.

"Believe me, there were a lot of suggestions about her disappearance. None of them dealt with an attack."

"I must have been out of the country. I don't remember a missing intern. And I would have if Gettys's name had been mentioned."

"It *was* about then," Colleen said.

She meant San Parrano. So...eight months ago.

"What kind of suggestions?"

"Nothing I can remember with a lot of detail. Not without doing some back-checking on the media stories. I can tell you that all of them were pretty unsavory."

"Exactly how unsavory?"

"Let me ask around. It's been a while. At the time I wasn't particularly interested in what happened to Gettys's associates. Maybe my feelings about the senator have colored my memory of the incident."

"You're leaving me in the dark here, Colleen," he accused. He recognized evasion when he heard it, especially from someone who usually shot as straight as his sister did. "That could be dangerous."

"I don't think she's a danger to what you're doing, Michael. I didn't mean to imply that."

You might have if you'd seen her with that knife.

"I was planning to get her to help me," he said, blocking the image of those sapphire eyes slowly filling with tears. "Without telling her who I'm working for, of course."

"Are you sure that's a smart move?"

"She's been here a while. We seem to have a mutual interest in finding out about what's going on. Would what you heard preclude her from working with me?"

There was a hesitation before Colleen answered. "Not necessarily."

"So you *do* remember the basics of those unsavory rumors," he said, trying to pin her down. They were probably nothing compared to the things he was beginning to imagine, none of which he liked. And none of which he could believe the woman he'd discovered today might be associated with. "What are we talking about? Drugs, spying, embezzlement?"

There was another silence. Michael was beginning to wonder if he'd lost the connection when Colleen said, "It was something about a call-girl ring."

A peculiar sensation tightened his stomach. Of course, just because Nicki Carson looked like a child when her eyes glazed with tears didn't mean she was an innocent. Few people were these days. Especially not women who worked for Franklin Gettys, a notorious womanizer.

"Political?" he asked, fighting other unwanted images.

"Men influential in government circles linked with ambitious young women, most of whom had some interest in politics," his sister confirmed.

He had to force his mind, still trapped by the remembrance of Nicki's body under his, to focus on what Colleen was saying.

"I can call some people," Colleen went on. "Get more details."

"She left town because she got caught? Or because she threatened to blow the whistle on someone?"

"At least one of the tabloids suggested she'd been permanently silenced because she had tapes of her clients. Most of the stories were more in the line of her running before she could be indicted for blackmail."

"And there's no question she was involved?"

"Supposedly she was in all of it. Up to her very pretty neck. I have some contacts among the Washington press. Jeremy Canton for one. He covered the story. I'm not sure he ever speculated on why Nicki left town," Colleen said. "I don't know who the source was for the call girl explanation, but I can try to find out from him. Are you saying she's been at the ranch since she disappeared?"

"She says she thought of hiding here because she figured it was the last place Gettys would look. And because she believed she could find out why that document she saw was important enough to make someone try to kill her."

"So her version has nothing to do with sex, lies *or* videotapes?"

"Hers has to do strictly with Gettys's ownership of the Half Spur."

Another silence. This time he knew the cause. Colleen

was digesting the information he'd just given her, trying to fit it into the framework in which Colorado Confidential was working.

"Do *you* think she's telling the truth?" she asked.

He avoided an answer. "How long will it take you to get in touch with Canton?"

"Give me a couple of days."

A couple of days. Despite the sickness in the pit of his stomach, Michael knew he didn't have a choice.

"No word on the baby?" he asked, changing the subject. He knew that she would have told him had there been.

"Nothing. I can't begin to imagine what the Langworthys must be feeling. Holly, the mother, has gone into seclusion. The press is foaming at the mouth for a chance to talk to her. It seems that when the family discovered the baby was missing, she said something about it all being her fault."

"A fairly natural reaction," Michael said. "Any mother would feel a certain amount of guilt if her child disappeared, no matter what the circumstances were."

"Granted, but in a kidnapping that has this much media interest, you can guess at the speculation that statement has set off."

He wondered briefly if that same kind of inches-and-airtime-to-fill conjecture had played a role in what had been written after Nicola Carson's disappearance. And then dismissed the idea as wishful thinking.

"I'll call you back in a few days," he said aloud. "I'd like to have any information you can dig up about Nicki Carson."

"I'll ask around, but remember that in her case, just as in Holly Langworthy's, media theory isn't the same thing as fact."

"Nor is every self-serving story someone tells to explain their actions."

"You liked her."

Past tense. He had, but he wondered what his sister had heard in his voice that had led her to that conclusion.

"She has guts. She thought I was the guy who'd attacked her. That he'd tracked her here. She pulled a knife on me."

Colleen laughed, which made him feel marginally better.

"What'd you do?"

Lay on top of her as she trembled because she thought she was about to die.

"I protected myself."

"I'm glad," Colleen said softly. "Keep on doing that. And call me in a couple of days. I'll see if I can have some more information for you then."

This time she broke the connection. He punched the off button and laid the phone on his stomach. He should get up and put it on the charger, but the pain medication was finally beginning to kick in. If he moved, it would negate the effects.

Why the hell had he thought he could do this? Shawn Jameson had been right, and he'd been too stubborn, or too stupid, to realize it.

He had come back to this trailer the last two nights feeling like he'd taken a beating. And far more important than his physical shortcomings, he had apparently lost the one instinct necessary for undercover work—the one that was supposed to tell him who he could trust.

He had believed Nicki Carson today. And Colleen had been right. Nicki's version had included nothing about being a whore for the rich and famous.

He didn't have many illusions left, certainly not about what went on in Washington. He'd seen too much of the slimy underbelly of this nation's politics. He had even been involved in some of it. More than he liked to remember.

And after all, was there really any difference in those who sold their souls for an ideology and those who sold their bodies for…?

For what? he wondered. Fun or profit? Just a small town girl trying to make good?

He put his crossed wrists over his forehead, closing his eyes. At the back of them, burned like the afterimage from a flashbulb's explosion, a pair of blue eyes looked into his as if he represented her last chance for salvation.

Not me, sweetheart. Believe me, I'm nobody's idea of a hero. Not even someone like you.

SINCE HE HADN'T BEEN able to sleep after the phone conversation with his sister, he had decided that tonight was as good a time as any to do a little reconnaissance around the place. There was a half moon and plenty of drifting clouds, the kind that provide shadows to disguise and distort movement.

He had skirted behind the row of trailers, which were spaced equidistant from one another on a wide semicircle along the outward perimeter of the compound. He knew, because he had asked her, that Nicki occupied the one directly in front of the cabin, although several hundred yards up the ridge.

She had also been able to provide the names of the hands who lived in the others. Not that it seemed necessary for him to know that tonight. There wasn't a soul stirring in the postmidnight stillness.

Somewhere in the distance a coyote howled, the sound far more mournful than that made by its domesticated cousin. Mating or hunting? With clouds periodically obscuring the moon, it was the perfect night for predators.

Even for has-been predators, he thought with a smile. So far, however...

Maybe because he had still been concentrating on the distant yowl, only gradually did he become aware of another sound, fainter than the first and more foreign to this environment. As he listened, the distant pop of rotor blades grew louder.

After a few seconds it became obvious that the chopper was heading in this direction. Maybe a military flight or a rescue operation. Whatever it was, the thing sounded as if it would pass right over the ranch.

As that thought formed, the helicopter appeared atop the south ridge. It flew over the cabin in the center of the compound, a solid black shape against the lesser darkness of the sky. If it bore any identifying markings, Michael couldn't see them from here.

His eyes followed the chopper as it passed above his head. He half expected the inhabitants of the trailers to come outside, but the helicopter was fairly high. If they were asleep, they probably wouldn't be disturbed by the low thrum of its blades.

Only when it disappeared behind the opposite ridge did Michael begin to move again. He had intended to explore the area behind the trailers simply to familiarize himself with the terrain. He had had no opportunity to do that during the daytime. Besides, betraying an interest in the topography would almost certainly make Quarrels suspicious.

He could still hear the sound of the chopper as he made his way behind the trailer Nicki had indicated belonged to Ralph Mapes. And the one after that—

He realized suddenly that the sound of the rotor had stopped. It hadn't faded into silence—it had been cut off. As if someone had shut down the power.

He strained to filter out the other night noises and focus

solely on that one, but the distinctive sound the chopper had made was completely gone. Since it hadn't faded off into the distance, the helicopter must have set down. Somewhere on the other side of the ridge behind him.

He needed to know what it was doing there. And as much as he hated to think about the prospect, there was really only one way he was going to find out.

He turned in the direction of the trailer where Nicola was sleeping. She would be able to climb more quickly than he to a vantage point from which the other side of the ridge could be seen. However, because of what Colleen had intimated, he was reluctant to wake her and ask for her help.

After he knew more, maybe, but not now. Not yet. This was his job. An assignment he'd accepted. For all the wrong reasons, he admitted, but accepted nonetheless.

If he could get up there before the chopper took off, well and good. If not, then one of the troubling questions that had kept him from sleep tonight, the one about his ability to handle this job, would be answered.

THE BRIGHT SPILL of moonlight spotlighted two men working below. The clearing on the top of the escarpment where they were was small, barely large enough to hold both the helicopter and Quarrels's pickup. It did, however, have the advantage of being relatively inaccessible. The foreman would have had to take his truck off-road to reach it.

Michael had picked his way up and across the ridge behind the trailers, moving as quickly as he could. And he knew he would pay the price for that frantic climb tomorrow.

As he crouched to watch the scene below, his legs trembled with exhaustion. His breathing was harsh and uneven, and the normal dull ache in his knee had become a fire. He must be more out of shape from the months he'd spent in the hospital and rehab than he'd realized, but at least he was here.

And so were they. Still here, despite the time it had taken him to work his way to the top of the ridge.

He wished he had night-vision goggles or even a pair of binoculars. Since he didn't, he concentrated on anything that might allow him to identify the man who was helping Quarrels unload the truck.

From this distance it was impossible to see the man's face, but by comparing his size to the foreman's, Michael could make an assessment of his height and build. Shorter than Quarrels's six feet, and slighter.

As he watched, another distinguishing feature became apparent. There was a hesitation in his stride as he crossed and recrossed the path between the pickup and the chopper. Even if Michael couldn't identify him any other way, that distinctive limp might be important in recognizing the pilot at some later date.

If he could get closer, he might be able to read the tail numbers on the chopper. Colleen, with her contacts, could use them to identify the recipient of the blood samples they'd taken yesterday. Maybe that would give them an idea of the scope and legitimacy of the research project in which the Half Spur was involved.

Despite the continued protest from his knee, he began to make his way carefully down the side of the ridge. He selected the next boulder or outcropping or bush that could provide cover before he made his noiseless descent to it.

Periodically he paused, checking on the progress of the team below, making sure they were still working and hadn't been alerted to his presence. So far, so good.

Then, as he moved toward his next position, his boot dislodged a stone, hardly more than a pebble, and sent it ricocheting down the rock face. Thankfully it was small, so that the noise wasn't loud enough to reach the ears of the men loading the boxes into the chopper.

Just as he was congratulating himself on the narrow escape, he realized that theirs was not the most sensitive hearing on the mountain tonight. Quarrels had brought one of the Border collies with him, maybe for such a contingency as this. The animal, which had been lying unseen in the shadow cast by the pickup, came to life as the stone bounced off the lower slope. It sprang to its feet, hackles raised, nose pointing upward to Michael's hiding place.

The first frenzied barks of alarm subsided into a low, throaty growl while Michael pressed himself flat against the rock he'd been attempting to leave. He waited, hardly daring to breathe.

Quarrels's voice was raised in question, although Michael couldn't distinguish all the words. Then there was a long, pregnant silence. All the while the collie continued to growl.

Would they come up here? Or would the foreman abandon the unloading to drive back to the compound to conduct a bed check of his employees? And if he did, could Michael get back down there before Quarrels did?

The dog had already told them something was up here. The chance they would put his warning down to some natural predator wasn't one Michael could afford to take. He needed to move now, while they were still occupied with deciding what to do.

He began to back away from the boulder where he was hiding, careful to keep it between him and the two men. When he reached his previous place of concealment, he paused for a few seconds to listen.

The dog's growling had stopped. There was no sound from the clearing below, which might mean they were doing the same thing he was doing—waiting and listening.

He retreated again, using the same areas of cover he'd employed on the way down. Despite the burn in his knee and the fact that he was climbing, he was still moving faster than he had coming down because he was being less cautious. They were either going to dismiss the dog's warning or come up here to investigate. In either case, he couldn't see that he had anything to gain by staying put. He needed to get back to the trailer in case Quarrels came calling. If Quarrels did decide to do that, the pickup gave him an advantage that would be hard to negate.

He reached the top of the ridge, keeping low so he wouldn't be outlined against the moonlight. He didn't stop to look back down at the escarpment, but hurried down the slope leading back to the semicircle of trailers.

Behind him he heard the rotor of the helicopter begin to turn. If the chopper was leaving, the foreman wouldn't be far behind. He began to hurry even more, half-sliding and half-running, ignoring the agony each jarring step sent into the damaged muscles and bones of his knee.

Then, warned by the increasing whine of the engine, Michael threw himself flat as the helicopter roared over the top of the ridge, its ominous black shadow above him. It hovered low enough to kick up dust and debris from the ground around him, its sound deafening. Obviously they were no longer making any effort to hide the chopper's presence from the sleeping compound.

He knew the pilot was searching for him. He could only be thankful the guy didn't have a light.

The helicopter made a series of passes back and forth over the top of the ridge. After hovering futilely over the slope for a few minutes, the helicopter nosed down and then lifted, heading off to the south.

As its noise faded, Michael became aware of another, even more troubling. Quarrels's pickup, its engine revved high to pull some incline, could clearly be heard from the other side of the ridge.

He scrambled up and continued his reckless descent, gritting his teeth with each hobbling step. He had no idea what the foreman would do if he discovered he wasn't in his trailer, but it was certain his usefulness as an investigator on the Half Spur would be over.

In the time he'd spent here, the only things he'd discovered were that they flew the blood samples out—which was not exactly earth-shattering information—and that Franklin Gettys's former intern was hiding out on the place. And he couldn't see how either piece of information related to a kidnapped baby.

When he finally reached the bottom of the ridge, he began to sprint toward his trailer. He could no longer hear Quarrels's truck, not over his own gasping breathing. As he ran, he kept glancing toward the center of the compound, trying to see if the pickup was parked there.

It wasn't. Apparently, despite his leg, he'd made it down before the foreman had been able to drive the distance around the ridge.

All he had to do was get inside and take his clothes off. If Quarrels did come calling, no matter what he suspected, he would have no proof.

He stepped up on the high step that led to the trailer, opening the door he hadn't bothered to lock when he'd left. The resultant squeak of metal against metal seemed to echo in the stillness.

He slipped in, lifting the door away from the threshold before he eased it closed. Then he stood in the darkness, straining to hear the sound of the pickup.

Instead, in the dark silence of his trailer, his own breathing suspended as he listened, what he heard was the distinct sound of someone else's.

Cade Wasson

Chapter Eight

Nicki clicked on the penlight she'd brought, directing its beam toward the door that had just opened and then closed. Michael Wellesley put his hand up to shield his eyes.

"Did you hear it?" she asked. "A helicopter. It was so loud I thought it was going to land in the middle of the compound."

"Shh."

He lowered his hand, eyes still narrowed against the light. He turned his head, obviously listening for something. She waited, listening too, and heard nothing.

"Michael?"

Without answering, he made a motion with his hand, again warning her to silence. After a moment she heard what he had obviously been listening for. The sound of a car, its tires crunching over the mix of chert and gravel the ranch roads were made of.

"Quarrels," Michael explained. "He's probably coming here."

"Did he see you?"

"He heard me. I was checking out the chopper. You need to go back to your trailer. He'll probably wake everybody to see if he can figure out which of us was outside."

She started toward the door, but he didn't move out of

her way. Instead he assumed the same position he had before. Completely intent on whatever was happening outside. This time the sound was much clearer. And much closer.

The car, or rather the truck, if this were indeed Quarrels, was obviously heading up the road that led here. Together, as if frozen, they followed the sound of its approach.

Then, like a nightmare, headlights played over the windows of the trailer, which were on the same side as the door. There was no chance she could get out unseen.

The pickup pulled up in front. Before Quarrels could shut off the engine, Michael had closed the distance between them, grabbing her shoulders and using them to propel her toward the bathroom. He put his mouth against her ear before he released her.

"Kill the light. Get into the shower enclosure and stay there no matter what happens."

Fingers shaking, she pressed the off button on the miniature flashlight. As soon as she had, he let her go with a small shove, moving away into the darkness behind her.

She fumbled her way toward the bathroom. Behind her she could hear a series of faint thumps from the area near the bed. Michael taking off his clothing and dropping the items onto the floor, she realized, obviously to try and make it appear as if he'd been asleep.

Outside, the door of the truck slammed. It was all the impetus needed to make her take that final step. She slipped into the shower stall and silently eased the door closed behind her. The bed in the other room creaked under Michael's weight.

She leaned back against the cool vinyl wall. She squeezed her eyelids shut, trying to control the sound of her breathing. Trying to prepare for what was about to happen.

Still, she jumped when whoever was outside began to

pound on the door, the blows so strong they shook the
entire trailer. She opened her eyes in the musty darkness,
waiting for Michael's response.

For what seemed an eternity there was none. Not until
that forceful knocking, louder than before, sounded again.
This time she heard the creak of the bed and felt the trailer
vibrate as Michael walked across to the door.

"Who is it?"

A reasonable question. His voice as he asked it had be-
trayed nothing beyond a legitimate concern and the desire
for information. The answer, muffled but intelligible, was
four words.

"It's Quarrels. Open up."

*Refuse. Tell him it's the middle of the night. Tell him to
come back in the morning. Tell him anything, but don't let
him in here.*

Anxiety building, she pressed her spine against the side
of the enclosure as if she could somehow melt into it. It
would be one thing for Nicola Carson to be found in a
man's trailer after midnight. It would be quite another for
Nate Beaumont to be discovered there.

She had been so careful all these months to do nothing
that might draw attention to herself. Hiding out in the one
place she believed Gettys would never in a million years
think to look for her. Then tonight she had taken a foolish
chance, which had brought her to this. All because Michael
Wellesley had promised to help her.

She heard the sound of the outer door being opened with
the same metallic squeal her own always made.

"Something wrong?" Michael's voice, its tone again
perfect. Calm. Believable.

"You been out?"

"Out?"

"Outside. You been outside tonight, McAdams?"

"I've been *asleep* tonight. What the hell's going on?"

"Hear anything?" Quarrels demanded, ignoring Michael's question.

"Like what?"

There was a telltale hesitation. Apparently Quarrels didn't want to talk about the helicopter, especially if there was any possibility Michael hadn't heard it.

"Somebody moving around."

"Outside? If they were, they didn't wake me. Want me to help you look?"

Another pause, this one slightly more prolonged.

"Probably nothing," Quarrels said grudgingly. "I'll ride around before I turn in. Take a look-see at everything."

"Something I should worry about?"

"Guess I'm just jumpy. Too much empty space around here. Gets you anxious. 'Specially at night. Sorry to bother you."

"It's okay. Give a yell if you want some help searching."

"I can handle it."

Nicki wasn't sure that the confrontation, anticlimactic as it had been, was over until she heard the truck door slam again. She waited, unmoving, until the engine caught, and then she heard the distinctive noise of the pickup's wheels moving over the gravel.

She had already reached for the handle of the enclosure door when it was pushed inward. Instinctively, she raised the penlight and clicked it on.

Michael stood outside the shower stall, looking in at her. There was something in his expression that she didn't understand.

"Is he gone?"

"Come on," he said. "You've got to get out of here. He could be headed for your place."

He turned and went back into the bedroom. Confused, she stepped over the edge of the stall and followed him. Without any explanation, he walked to the outside door and opened it, standing inside the threshold to look out.

She could clearly see his shape, his shoulders filling the narrow span of the opening. Using the moonlight behind him as a guide, she walked over to the door to wait for his signal that she should make her run.

She was close enough that the scent of his body surrounded her. A hint of the soap he'd used in his shower tonight. Or maybe his shampoo. It was pleasantly masculine in any case.

Underlying that commercial fragrance was something far more subtle. The salt-tang of clean skin that has been touched by perspiration. Obviously the result of his evasion of the chopper, the scent was the faint, nearly sensual smell of an athlete after a hard workout.

Or of a lover, exhausted and sated.

"Now?" she asked, fighting against the dangerous images it evoked.

The situation they were in didn't help with that struggle. She knew Michael had undressed before he lay down, pretending to be asleep. She didn't believe he'd had time to put his clothes back on before he'd opened the door to the shower.

She resisted the impulse to put out her hand and test her hypothesis. Would the tips of her fingers encounter warm, bare skin or the rough texture of the chamois shirt he'd been wearing earlier today?

"He's headed toward the compound," he said, breaking into that disturbing train of thought. They listened together as the sound of the truck faded away down the hill. "I guess I'm the only one he was worried about."

The comment held the edge of amused self-deprecation

she had enjoyed hearing in his voice this afternoon. Yesterday afternoon, she amended, realizing that it was almost dawn.

"You're the unknown," she said. "You're bound to be under suspicion when something happens."

There was no answer for a heartbeat, the words seeming to echo between them in the heated darkness.

"I talked to my boss tonight," he said.

The change of topic threw her. *Boss?* Obviously he didn't mean Quarrels, so... Whoever had sent him here?

"About the Half Spur?"

"Mostly about Nicola Carson."

There was something about the way he said her name that bothered her. Some undercurrent she didn't understand. Just like she didn't understand whatever had been in his face when he'd pushed the door of the shower enclosure open.

"About what I told you? The fax and Gettys? Or about the attack?"

"All of it," he said. "By the way, your disappearance got quite a bit of attention from the media. Did you know that?"

She had known there would be inquiries from her friends and especially from her mom. That there would be some newspaper coverage. The low-key kind that occurred whenever there was a missing person in a city that size.

She was hardly a celebrity. Her friends might put up posters and demand the D.C. police do something. In the end, she had accepted that the bureaucracy would grind on, and she'd be forgotten.

At first she had thought about notifying a couple of the people she cared about, people who cared about her, but finally she had decided it would be safer—maybe for them as well as for her—if no one knew anything. Coming to terms with the reality that her friends would be frantic with worry had actually been harder than making the decision to change her identity.

Thinking about her mom had been worse even than the long, lonely months she'd spent in hiding. Since her father's death, they'd been exceptionally close. While she was making her way west she had tried once to let her mother know she was alive. She hadn't dared risk anything as obvious as a birthday or Mother's Day card in case someone was watching her mom's mail, but she had mailed a blank "thinking of you" card, timed to arrive around her mom's anniversary. She had no idea if her mother had known it was from her.

"They must think I'm dead," she said softly. It was an old guilt, one she'd lived with a long time.

"Not all of them."

He was still facing the open doorway, although the red dots that were the taillights of Quarrels's truck had long since disappeared. The sound of its motor had also died away, leaving the darkness empty and silent. Except for the two of them.

"How do you know?" she asked.

He turned to face her, positioning himself, deliberately she believed, so that the moonlight slanting in through the open door behind him would illuminate her features and keep his shadowed.

"There were a couple of versions about why you left Washington. Only one of them dealt with the possibility of your demise."

When he didn't go on, it seemed he was waiting for a response, so she obliged. "And the other version?"

She genuinely wanted to know. The first few days there had been nothing in the papers, because it had taken a while for her absence to be noticed.

And then, as she'd traveled, she hadn't dared to call attention to herself. Not even by taking so small a risk as that involved in asking for the East Coast papers, which hadn't been readily available in those hole-in-the-wall bus stops she'd frequented.

Since she'd been here, of course, she'd had no way of keeping track of what was happening in Washington. Who she had been and what she had done there had become completely foreign to the world she now inhabited. A distant memory.

Instead of answering her question, Michael asked another she didn't understand.

"Did being Gettys's intern pay well?"

The note she hadn't liked was back in his voice. Mockery?

"I guess that depends on your perspective."

"Some of the Washington papers suggested you might have had plans to make a lot of money. Over and above your salary."

...a lot of money. Over and above your salary.

For a few seconds she had no idea what he meant. Not until she remembered her uneasiness with the senator's behavior.

"I wasn't planning on becoming the next Mrs. Gettys, if that's what they implied."

"Not the *Mrs.* at least. The senator's reputed to have an appreciation for women, especially beautiful ones who work for him. The younger they are, the better."

In other circumstances that might have been construed as a compliment. His tone kept her from believing he meant it as one.

"I wasn't planning to become his mistress either," she said coldly, "if that's what *you're* implying."

"I didn't think people called it that these days. A mistress. Of course, you'd be more familiar with the terminology than I would.''

"What is that supposed to mean?" she demanded, her temper beginning to flare.

"Did you have tapes of the senator himself? Or maybe just a few colleagues he wanted to control?"

"I don't have any idea what you're talking about."

She kept her voice low because her growing anger might make it strident. Neither of them could afford to attract attention to this clandestine meeting. It seemed he should be as conscious of that as she was.

"And you still claim you left Washington because you were attacked?"

"I told you what happened."

"Attacked because you saw a fax dealing with this property. A sheep farm."

"I don't *know* it was because of that," she said evenly. "It's the only thing I can think of that had made someone angry with me. An anger way out of proportion to what happened."

"I guess that's what bothers me," he said.

"Look—"

"Why would Gettys want to kill you for seeing a fax that related to this ranch?"

"Maybe if we can figure out what's going on here—"

"Or maybe someone was angry about something else you were doing," he interrupted her again. "Could that be it?"

She felt as if she were talking to a different person from the man who'd promised to help her. A man who had claimed to be on the side of the angels.

Maybe this was some kind of test. An interrogation technique designed to make her defend her story. She was willing to do that. She had nothing to hide.

"I told you that the incident with Gettys was the only thing I could think of," she said, trying to sound patient and cooperative. "I hadn't made anyone else angry that I was aware of. I tried *never* to give anyone a reason to be upset with me."

She had always done more than was required of her. She had been discreet and loyal. Her only sin, if there had been one, was in having too much ambition.

The sin of the angels. One of her English teachers had used that phrase. In relation to *Paradise Lost,* maybe? She couldn't remember the exact context, but she did remember the words.

And they were appropriate, she thought bitterly. She had gone to Washington with such grandiose dreams. Instead—

"How about your clients?" Michael asked. "Ever make one of them angry? By threatening them maybe?"

"My…*clients?*" she repeated, honestly bewildered.

"It might amuse you to know that I believed you this afternoon. They probably did, too. Maybe even Gettys. You really are very good."

This is insane. He's insane.

That thought, when it came, caused everything to fall into place. All that secret agent crap. How he was willing to help her without knowing anything about her. Even the part about being on the side of the angels.

Like an idiot, she had bought into all of it. So damn desperate to have someone to trust. Lonely and frightened enough to reveal herself to the first lunatic who didn't look or act like one.

After months spent at this place, she had thought she had a pretty good idea about the lunatic profile. Obviously she'd been wrong. Maybe *dead* wrong.

In spite of the danger, the primary emotion she felt as this played out wasn't fear, but a sickening disappointment.

Disappointment in him. With who and what she'd thought he was.

Without responding to the last of that increasingly bizarre list of accusations, she tried to push past Michael Wellesley—or whatever the hell his name was—to get through the door. Even if Quarrels were still roaming around, running into him would be better than this.

Michael didn't move. Instead, he put his arm across the doorway, blocking her exit. Running up against it, she discovered that she'd been right about the warmth of bare skin.

"Running away again, Nicki?"

His voice was as soft as when he'd whispered those hurried instructions in her ear. His breath feathered against her cheek, as pleasant as the fragrance of his body.

This close to him, whatever had made her trust him this afternoon drew her again, made her want to believe that he was everything he'd said he was.

"I told you the truth. I don't know what you're talking about. All that about clients and threats. While I was in Washington I worked for Senator Gettys. That's *all* I did."

"Just the good little intern."

"Not little. Not by anyone's standards. But I was very good at what I did. Maybe that's what Gettys was afraid of."

"Afraid of how *good* you were."

It was not a question, and the mockery was back.

She put both hands on his arm, feeling the rigid muscle beneath her palms. She pushed against it as hard as she could, trying to force her way by him.

She couldn't budge it. As she'd reminded him, she wasn't small. After the past few months of hard physical labor, she certainly wasn't weak. Yet she was getting nowhere.

Frustrated and furious, finally feeling the first stirrings of real fear, she demanded, "Let me go, damn you, or I swear I'll start screaming."

As soon as the words were out, she was ashamed of having said them. It was such a damn woman thing to say. It would serve her right if he laughed at her.

"Scream away," he said, calling that ridiculous bluff. "That should get Quarrels back here in a hurry."

The amusement she'd expected was in his voice, even if he hadn't laughed. She opened her mouth, without, of course, having any intention of screaming. She had far more to lose than he did if she were found here.

Before she could draw breath to fuel another idiotic threat, his head lowered, tilting at exactly the right angle to allow his mouth to settle over hers. Her lips had already been parted when his tongue invaded, hard and demanding.

There was nothing of the sweet, tentative exploration of a normal first kiss. This was insistent. Aggressive.

For a second or two, the shock of what he was doing held her motionless, unable to protest. As soon as that paralysis broke, she tried to pull her head back to escape the expert assault of his mouth.

His right hand, the one that wasn't occupied with blocking the door, locked around the back of her neck, holding her as his tongue continued to ravage. Her left hand lifted to his shoulder as she attempted to push him away.

He turned her instead, pressing her into the wall next to the doorway. The maneuver had been as quick as the one he'd used this afternoon to take her knife away. And just as practiced. The heat and strength of his body shocked her.

The arm that had guarded the opening was behind her now, his fingers, broad and hard, splayed over her lower spine. She continued to struggle. Using her hands, which were caught between their bodies, she pushed against his chest. And had as little success as when she had tried to break his hold across the door.

She felt his left hand slip downward, lifting her lower body. And then he bent his knees, lowering his own to meet it. She fought the surge of feeling that shivered through her at the intimate contact.

She had been wrong about his lack of clothing, she realized. At some time he'd slipped on the jeans he'd worn earlier. He hadn't bothered to zip them, but at least he was partially clothed.

Despite the jeans, there was no doubt about the strength of his arousal. He might be trying to intimidate her, but he couldn't hide his body's response.

He released her neck, the hand that had held it joining the other to cup under her buttocks, bringing her body into an even more intimate contact with his. Anger exploded in her brain.

She couldn't afford to scream for help, and he knew it. She had told him her secret, and now he was taking advantage of the fact that it would be far more dangerous for her to reveal that she was a woman.

She brought her arms straight up, jerking her head to the side. Since his fingers were no longer wrapped around her neck, she was able to free her mouth from the domination of his.

"What the hell are you *doing?*" she demanded.

Something, the sheer anger and bewilderment in her voice perhaps, or maybe the unexpected movement, stopped him. They were still eye-to-eye, their noses almost touching, but he made no move to put his lips over hers again.

He simply looked at her. As she watched, his face hardened, his mouth settling into a thin, straight line. After a moment he stepped back, releasing her.

She took a quick, hiccupping breath, waiting for whatever came next. Based on the speed of his reflexes, she knew that if she tried to cut for the door, he would catch her.

Catch her and then what? She couldn't be sure.

"What are you?"

His voice, whispering from the darkness, had been wiped clean of inflection. Slowly she shook her head, her eyes holding his in the moonlight from the open door.

What are you? Not who, but what.

Insane, she thought again, drawing another short, sobbing breath. She hadn't realized until then how long it had been since she'd remembered to breathe. She had forgotten everything but the feel of his mouth and his body moving against hers. Even now, even after what he'd done, her responses to that left her confused and unsettled.

"Why did you do that?"

Stupid question, she thought. He had done it because he was a man. Because he could. And yet somehow, that was too simple an answer for what had just happened. Too pat.

"To see what it's like."

"To *kiss* someone?"

"Someone like you. I probably couldn't have afforded you on my salary."

Clients. Afforded. Someone like you. The phrases were beginning to make some sort of twisted sense, although not in any relation to who she was. *What are you?* he had asked. Apparently he had already decided.

"*You* couldn't afford me on *any* salary," she said.

Coldly furious and humiliated, she waited for him to retaliate. Instead, as the silence stretched, he took another step back.

"Get out."

While you can. He didn't say it, but that's what she heard. Without bothering to try for a dignified exit, she turned and stumbled down the step. By the time she hit the ground, she was running.

Chapter Nine

He'd never manhandled a woman in his life. Until last night.

Sickened by the memory, Michael turned on the narrow, uncomfortable cot to face the windows. Although he had closed the blinds before he'd gone back to bed, sunlight streamed in between their narrow plastic slats, dimly lighting the room.

Thank God it was Sunday. He wasn't sure he could have managed if he'd had to get back on a horse today. Or stoop a few hundred times to take blood samples. Actually, he wasn't totally convinced he was up to getting out of bed. He found it reassuring to know he didn't have to.

Of course, he would have to at some time. Just as he would eventually have to face Nicola Carson. If for no other reason than to reassure her that whatever she'd done, and whatever *he'd* done, his offer of help was still on the table.

Whatever she'd done…

Why the hell did it bother him so much that a woman he barely knew wasn't as pure as the driven snow? Neither was he. Some of the things he'd been involved in with the agency would horrify Nicki Carson. And rightfully so. In comparison, all she'd done—

He blocked that thought, closing his mind to the images it created by trying to think of something else. Anything else.

The problem was that no matter what he started thinking about, he always ending up remembering what had happened between them. And he couldn't figure out why he couldn't put it out of his head.

Guilt, obviously. But there were other dimensions to what he was feeling. Things that had made him toss and turn restlessly long after Nicki left. Things that had awakened him this morning with a sense of regret and an aching head, the kind reminiscent of a bad hangover.

Maybe that's exactly what this was, he thought. Some kind of emotional hangover.

He had wanted to punish her for not being what he'd thought she was. For not living up to some cheesy scenario he'd composed on the spot yesterday afternoon.

She was the poor, sweet damsel in distress. A role he'd created for her so he could play knight errant. And as soon he discovered she didn't quite fit the part, he'd been pissed. Royally pissed.

Probably because he had been so strongly attracted to her. And that was the other thing he didn't understand.

Granted, she *was* female. Due to that botched mission to San Parrano and dealing with the aftereffects, he'd been without a woman for a long time. The way she dressed and that god-awful haircut, however, made it difficult to distinguish her womanly attributes.

Unless you're lying on top of them.

He ignored the unwanted reminder from his conscience, plowing on with his attempt to figure out why he felt the way he did. In no way, shape or form could Nicki Carson be considered his type. So what the hell kind of lapse in judgment made him want to condemn her for being a prostitute and want to kiss her at the same time?

Not only to kiss her.

If there was one thing he'd always taken pride in, it was being honest with himself. He had wanted her last night, in spite of what Colleen had told him. And if she had given any sign that she was agreeable—

Maybe that's what was throwing him, he conceded. The fact that she'd been persistent in her attempt to get away from him. Even when he'd felt her physical response.

Ego, old buddy? In spite of the sense of remorse gnawing at him, his lips curved in self-derision.

Could be. He had one. Most people who did what he'd done for a goodly portion of their lives had very healthy egos or they didn't survive. It was as simple as that.

He couldn't deny, not to himself at least, that he had wanted her pretty desperately. Despite the fact she was possibly a call girl. Despite that crack about him not being able to afford her price.

And clearly she hadn't wanted any part of him. So... maybe what he was feeling *was* bruised ego.

That didn't, however, explain away the things she'd said. Things that had echoed and reechoed in his consciousness throughout the remainder of the night. Even while he'd slept, the images of her eyes, filled with anger and confusion, had haunted him.

You couldn't afford me on any salary.

There seemed only one way to interpret that, but he knew in his gut he was missing something. Something that should be obvious.

Maybe he could figure it out if his head wasn't throbbing so hard that it had become difficult to think. He needed aspirin. A shower. Coffee. Not necessarily in that order.

He didn't have any idea how the dining hall functioned

on Sunday. He did have the pickup. There were a few things he needed in town anyway. He would get dressed and drive into Granby for breakfast if he'd missed it here by sleeping in.

While he was there, he'd call Colleen from a pay phone, a far more secure method than using his satellite phone. He had promised to give her a few days to track down the source of those stories about Nicki, but maybe she'd heard something by now. Worth a phone call.

He sat up and, putting his hand beneath the damaged knee, carefully swung his legs off the side of the bed. Every muscle in his body seemed to protest the movement. And once he was sitting upright, the ache in his head turned into a full-blown catastrophe.

Steeling himself, he put both hands on the mattress, preparing to push up off the bed and start the process of showering and getting dressed. Before he could, someone knocked on the door of the trailer.

This was nothing like Quarrels's banging. It was restrained, polite, almost apologetic. As if it wasn't intended to wake him if he weren't already up.

Nicki? He would have thought it'd be a cold day in hell before she'd come knocking on his door, but there was always the possibility he'd read her wrong last night.

"Just a minute," he called.

He reached down to the pile of clothing on the floor and grabbed the jeans he'd worn yesterday. Although the procedure wasn't pleasant, he got both feet into their narrow legs before he stood to pull them up and zip them. He didn't bother with the metal button at the waist.

As he crossed the narrow room, he held on to any object along the way that offered support for his knee. The pain in it rivaled the ache in his head.

"Who is it?" he asked, feeling a flicker of déjà vu.

"It's Mapes, Mac. Got a favor to ask."

Although he'd had little contact with the other hands during the past couple of days, other than those quick, nearly monastically silent meals, he remembered that Mapes was the only one who had introduced himself. He turned the lock on the door and pulled it open. It squealed unpleasantly, just as it had last night.

The old man had stepped down to the ground while he waited, faded Stetson in his hand. He squinted into the morning sunlight as he looked up at the doorway.

"Too early for you?" he asked.

"I was awake," Michael said.

"Missed you at breakfast. Figured you was sleeping in."

Which answered one of his questions. Apparently there was no relaxation of the dining hours because of the weekend. The coffee he so desperately needed would have to be obtained in Granby.

"Thought maybe you was planning on driving into town."

The question had been casually posed, but the dark eyes seemed eager. And after all, Mapes would be another source of information about what went on around here.

"I was," Michael confirmed. "You need a lift?"

"Be obliged to you. Ran out of smokes a couple of days ago. Been bumming, but folks are tired of it. Ain't saying they shouldn't be. Finally talked Charlie into a little advance, but he ain't going in this weekend. Thought maybe you was."

"I'll be leaving in about an hour. You're welcome to ride."

"Much obliged," the old man said again. "I'll just wait out here 'til you're ready to go. If you don't mind."

Michael hesitated, unable to remember what he'd done with the satellite phone last night. He also tried to picture anything inside the trailer that might reveal Nicki's visit. After a moment, he decided he could explain either of those away.

"You can wait in here if you want."

Mapes grinned, his leathery face creasing like an accordion. "Borrowed a couple more smokes at breakfast. I'll just stay out here and enjoy 'em. Ain't in no hurry now. You take your time."

"Suit yourself," Michael said.

The cowboy turned and walked over to the truck, putting his hat on as he did. When he reached the back of the pickup he glanced up at Michael again, head cocked in inquiry.

"Mind if I lower the tailgate to sit on?"

"Be my guest."

"I won't get no ashes in the bed."

"You can't hurt it. Do whatever you like, Ralph. I won't be long."

"Much obliged."

Michael watched as the old man let down the tailgate and then hoisted himself onto it. He took a cigarette out of the pocket of his shirt and moistened its length with his tongue, as if he'd rolled it himself. He lit it, cupping the match in his gnarled hand, and then took a deep drag, releasing the smoke into the morning air.

Satisfied that his guest was occupied, Michael stepped back inside the trailer, closing the door behind him. As he did, he realized that he was standing exactly where he'd stood last night when he'd kissed Nicki.

Maybe that was something else that shower would do, he thought as he limped toward the bathroom. Maybe it would wash the taste of her lips and the feel of her body out of his head.

If it didn't, he was in for a long, unpleasant day.

"I'M NOT SAYING Charlie's no bad boss, you understand. Just ornery. Likes having things his way. 'Course when you're the boss, you get to expect that. I've shore worked for a heap 'a worser men.''

The old man seemed happy to talk without much prodding. The sheer isolation of the Half Spur, even among the people who worked there, could account for that. During the trip into Granby, however, Michael had come to the realization that Mapes was naturally gregarious, which suited him fine. The cowboy's need for a ride to town was proving fortuitous.

"He got a temper?" Michael asked.

"Can have. I've seen him fly off the handle a couple of times."

"How long you been here, Ralph?"

"Going on five months. I reckon me and the kid are vying for some kind of record for the Spur," he said with a thin, high-pitched chuckle. "Folks shore don't stay there long."

"Accommodations or the isolation?"

"Both, maybe. Food ain't nothing to write home about either. Suits me all right, you understand. I got me one of them cast-iron stomachs."

"You can get a good meal in town today." As he said it, Michael wondered if the advance that would provide the old man his "smokes" would stretch to cover anything else. "I'm buying. As long as you'll keep me company while we eat it," he added.

"Ain't no call for that. I owe you for the ride."

"I was coming in anyway. I'm glad to have you. It gets lonely up there."

"Ain't that the truth. The one I feel sorry for is the kid."

"How's that?"

"Nobody his age. No women around, if you take my

meaning. No transportation. Quarrels rides him 'cause he knows the kid'll take it.''

''Rides him?''

''Worst jobs. Things none of us likes to do, but we're used to. I don't think the kid is.''

If what Colleen had told him was true, Nicola Carson wouldn't be used to ranch work. Given her background, it seemed strange that she was so proficient at the tasks he'd seen her perform. Of course, she'd had several months to learn the ropes, but considering what the old man had just said, he wouldn't think Quarrels would have been patient enough to keep her on if she hadn't had some clue about the work when she arrived.

''Like taking those blood samples?'' Michael asked, trying to steer the conversation into the area he needed information about.

He didn't want to think about how Nicki Carson, high-priced Washington call girl, had learned to be a ranch hand so quickly. It might force him to reevaluate his assessment of her. Just as he didn't want to hear the old man's sympathy for the life she was leading. Not this morning at any rate.

''Ain't quite figured those out myself,'' Mapes said.

''You mean why we take them?''

''What they're doing with them.''

''I think Quarrels takes them somewhere.''

''Nope. They got a place right here.''

''They?''

''Government. Whoever's running this shebang.''

''He takes the samples into Granby?''

Because he'd seen them loaded onto a helicopter last night, Michael knew Mapes's information was faulty, but it might be helpful to learn why the old man thought the nearby town was the destination of those blood samples.

"Not in Granby. I mean they got a place on the ranch. Some kind of lab."

"Are you telling me there's a research lab on the Half Spur?"

If Mapes was right, then this whole thing was more bizarre than he'd thought. Something that certainly would warrant further investigation.

"*Some* kind a lab. Don't you say nothing to nobody, now, about me telling you. We ain't supposed to know."

Obviously whatever facility the cowboy was talking about wasn't within the central compound. Michael had been inside every structure there, and there was nothing that could by any stretch of the imagination be construed as a lab. According to both Nicki and Quarrels, someone was living in each of the trailers, which probably meant they weren't being used for experiments.

"It must be pretty well hidden away," Michael suggested.

"In a place that most folks don't know is even part of the Spur. Charlie likes it that way."

"Somewhere up in the mountains?"

"There's lots of territory up there, if you think about it. More than a couple thousand sheep could ever need."

Michael knew there were several upland pastures. Without Nicki's guidance yesterday, he would have had no clue where they were taking that part of the flock.

He really needed to do some exploring, like that he'd begun last night when the helicopter arrived. Apparently he couldn't limit it to the area around the compound.

"You been there? To the lab?" He glanced toward his right to catch a glimpse of the old man's face.

"Not me. Friend of mine who worked on the Spur stumbled onto it by accident."

"He still around?"

"Took off a couple 'a days later. Guess he didn't like the idea of there being some kind of secret facility on the place. I ain't too wild about it myself, but as long as it's up there and we're down at the compound, I don't let it bother me too much."

"And you think that lab's got something to do with the blood samples?"

"Makes sense, don't it? I just figured that's where Charlie took 'em. Could be somewhere else. I've not seen the place, mind you. Just hearsay from my friend."

Michael assumed Mapes was using friend as a euphemism for a fellow hired hand. There seemed to be little true friendship on the ranch.

"So what'd your friend say about it? He tell you what it's like?"

"Didn't seem inclined to talk about it. 'Course Gene never was very talkative, so that ain't surprising."

"Gene?"

"Gene Orbock. The one that found the lab I was telling you about."

"You know how he happened to find it?"

The old man didn't answer for a moment. His lips pursed as he considered the winding mountain two-lane ahead of them.

"You been decent to me," Mapes said. "Bringing me into town and all. Hate to see you get into trouble. So I'm gonna give you a friendly warning. You leave stuff like that lab alone. Charlie don't like people nosing around up there."

"You think he fired your friend because he saw it?"

Another long hesitation.

"Maybe. Maybe Gene just decided to leave on his own. Or maybe—"

The words were abruptly cut off. When Michael took his

eyes off the road to look at Mapes, the old man's lips were pressed together as if he were deliberately holding something in.

"Maybe what, Ralph?"

"I always wondered why he left without saying goodbye. It wasn't like him, you know. Not just to go off without a word."

If Mapes was suggesting what Michael thought he might be, then there was more going on at the Half Spur than he or Colleen had imagined. Maybe Nicki's instinct that the cause of that attack in Washington had something to do with this ranch was a valid one. Assuming, of course, there had been an attack in the first place.

And with what he had just heard in the old man's voice as he'd talked about his friend's disappearance, that seemed to be more of a possibility than it had last night.

Chapter Ten

He was going to have to apologize some time. The longer Michael thought about what had happened last night, the more convinced he'd become of that.

He'd always been of the "rip the bandage off the wound" school. Once he made up his mind that this was the right thing to do, he was eager to get it over with. Or maybe, he admitted as he walked toward Nicki's trailer, that eagerness was something else entirely. Something he didn't want to think about.

He had waited until a couple of hours after dark before he opened his door. The betraying squeak of metal against metal had been the only sound in the stillness. Taking that as a sign that most people had settled in for the night, he had again cut through the aspens in back of the trailers. Noiselessly, he skirted the one that belonged to Mapes, situated between his and Nicki's.

The main generator was still operating, so the lights were on. Although he seriously doubted anybody was paying attention to who was out visiting on the Half Spur, his encounter with Quarrels last night and the story Ralph had told him today made him reluctant to take a chance on being seen approaching Nicki's door.

If Quarrels *was* suspicious of him because of last night,

he couldn't afford to let that suspicion spread to her. That ridiculous disguise wouldn't stand up to any kind of serious examination.

The only reason she'd managed to carry it off this long was the lack of interaction among the hands and her uncanny ability to fade into the wallpaper. Letting the foreman find out that the two of them had become allies would almost certainly change that. If the hand who'd discovered the lab hadn't left of his own free will, as Mapes had seemed to imply, then neither he nor Nicki could afford to let anyone know they were interested in the operation of the ranch.

When he arrived at Nicki's trailer, he forced himself to wait in the shadows of the trees through five long minutes just to be sure he hadn't been followed. As he listened to the subtle night noises around him, he could hear music coming from the trailer Mapes occupied. Some country station, faint enough that it wouldn't mask other sounds of human activity. There simply weren't any.

Occasionally the smell of cigarette smoke drifted to him. The old man was apparently enjoying the purchase he'd made in town today, maybe as much as he had seemed to enjoy the meal they'd shared at an all-you-can-eat Sunday buffet. The fact that Ralph felt free enough to be smoking in his trailer, an act strictly against the rules, relieved a little of Michael's anxiety about the possibility that the foreman made night rounds.

At the end of the time he'd set to wait, he stepped out of the woods and tapped lightly on the window at the back of Nicki's trailer. Then he deliberately planted himself beneath it, illuminated by the light filtering through the grimy glass.

After a few seconds, Nicki appeared in the frame. He

pointed to the stand of trees behind him. Mouth tight, she shook her head and disappeared.

And what the hell did you expect?

He rapped on the window again, louder this time. Almost before he could lower his hand, it opened.

"What?" The tone of the question—hostile, demanding and too loud—made it clear his actions last night had destroyed any rapport they might have established the day before.

What *did* he want? To warn her about what Mapes had said, of course, but more importantly, to try and restore the trust he'd squandered when he'd kissed her. If that was possible.

Besides, he needed Nicki Carson. He needed her knowledge of how this place worked. That was the reason he had felt he had to come tonight, despite the danger.

"To say I'm sorry, for starters," he whispered, hoping she'd follow suit. "And to promise you that won't happen again."

He didn't know what she'd been expecting, but judging by her face it had clearly not been that.

"What made you think you had any right to touch me?"

A straightforward question about an action he had hoped to gloss over with an apology and his promise not to make that same mistake again. She didn't intend to let him off that lightly.

"Bad judgment?" he suggested. As he said it, he realized it was so obviously the truth that he had to work to keep any hint of amusement out of the question. "Come out and let me explain. All I'm asking is five minutes. It's too dangerous for us to talk here."

Without giving her a chance to refuse, he stepped back into the darkness, making his way into the heart of the thicket. He had no idea whether or not she'd come. He couldn't blame her if she didn't.

When the light inside the trailer went out, he took a breath, enormously relieved. He didn't want to have to talk to her in any of the public areas of the ranch, but if she hadn't agreed to meet him, he would have had to. She was too important to this investigation for him not to make the effort to set things right.

Although she made as little noise as possible, he had a few seconds warning of her approach. "Over here," he whispered, stepping out of the shadows to allow her to locate him.

She had dressed as she usually did, in those baggy, masculine garments. The subtle play of moonlight over her features made him wonder again how she'd ever carried this off. They were delicate, so obviously feminine he felt like a fool for having been taken in, even briefly.

"Bad judgment I'll buy," she said, picking up without any preliminaries the conversation they'd begun under her window. "What I want to know is what happened between yesterday afternoon and last night to *change* your judgment. You didn't try anything like that then, not even when we were..."

She didn't finish the sentence, clamping her lips closed as if she were embarrassed by what had happened yesterday afternoon. He understood what she meant, of course. He hadn't tried to kiss her, not even when he was lying on top of her. Last night, after talking to Colleen, he had.

Maybe she deserved to hear the truth about why he'd done that. Or maybe he just wanted to know what she had to say about the things his sister had told him.

"I found out why you left Washington." More of that rip-it-off-and-damn-the-pain mentality.

"*I* told you why I left Washington."

"And then I heard a different version."

"From who?"

"The people I work for."

A beat of silence.

"I don't think you ever told me who those people are."

"No, I didn't."

"And you aren't going to now," she said, reading his tone.

"That's something I'm not at liberty to disclose."

"How convenient." The words were edged with sarcasm.

"Actually, I was thinking that right now it's pretty damned *inconvenient*."

"Okay, if you don't want to talk about who you work for, why don't we talk about their version of my departure. Since it seems to have made such a difference in your attitude."

Get it over with. Maybe she really does have some explanation.

"According to them you had videotapes of some of Washington's power brokers in compromising situations, and you threatened to use them. *That's* why you had to leave town without a forwarding address."

"What kind of situations?" she asked, going straight to the salient part of the accusation. "Something criminal? Like taking a bribe?"

He could read nothing in her voice but curiosity. No guilt. No evidence of discomfort at the introduction of what he'd expected to be a highly uncomfortable topic.

Of course, it was possible she wasn't bothered by what she'd done. Or, as unlikely as it seemed, maybe Colleen's memory had been faulty. When he'd called his sister from the pay phone in Granby, she hadn't yet heard back from any of the people she'd contacted about the sources of that story.

Despite the seed of doubt Nicki's reaction was creating, he didn't see any option but to finish this. If she had lied to him, no matter the reason, it would adversely affect their working together. There seemed only one way to find that out.

"Situations of a sexual nature," he said.

She said nothing for a moment, but her lips parted in what looked like genuine shock.

"Let me get this straight. According to the people you work for I'm supposed to have had videotapes of influential people in *sexual* situations?"

The tone was exactly right. Not outrage, but confusion. Puzzlement. A hint of disbelief.

"Tapes which you threatened to use."

"For blackmail." Clarification rather than a question.

"That was the implication in the stories after your disappearance."

"Are you saying this was in the *papers?*"

"Most of them."

She closed her mouth, swallowing hard. That bothered her, which made him wonder for the first time about her family.

Maybe that was something Colleen should check out. Nicki Carson's family.

"And where, *supposedly,* did I get these tapes?"

"*Supposedly,*" he said, picking up her word and emphasizing it even more, "you were part of a call-girl ring that operated at the highest levels in Washington."

She laughed. From shock, maybe. It was devoid of amusement in any case. "Then I have to tell you—I don't think much of your sources."

With her denial, the tightness in his chest eased. He had

wanted her to deny it, he realized. And now that she had, he wanted to believe her. That was something else that had never happened to him before. Being unable to judge whether someone was telling the truth, simply because he very much wanted them to be.

"They're very reliable," he said aloud.

"Not in this case. I told you what happened. I know it doesn't make a lot of sense, but that's what happened. That's all that happened. This other—" She shook her head, the swing of cropped hair visible in the darkness. "They're making it up. Or they've mistaken me for someone else."

Was that a possibility? he wondered. What if this were all some kind of misunderstanding? Colleen had warned him she didn't remember all the details, and yet he'd gone off half-cocked. That wasn't like him. For some reason, he hadn't been able to discount emotionally what his sister had suggested. Despite that lack of certainty.

"That's possible."

"Thank you for the concession," she said. There was no doubt her gratitude was less than sincere.

"If I was wrong, I'm sorry. At the time I had no reason to doubt my sources. They *are* reliable."

"You know, I don't really give a damn what you choose to believe, but if that *is* what was reported in the papers, at least it proves one thing."

"I don't understand."

"I worried that I was wrong. Worried that maybe the man who attacked me *wasn't* trying to kill me. That it was just another mugging. But if people thought I was doing *that*—blackmailing people with videotapes—then I guess there's nothing very mysterious at all about why someone would want me dead, is there?"

"ORBOCK. GENE ORBOCK. I remember him," Nicki said, picturing in her mind the hand Mapes had mentioned. "He and Ralph did seem to be friendly, as unusual as that is around here. Then one morning he just wasn't here. You shouldn't make too much of that, by the way. That's not unusual.''

"A lot of turnovers?'' Michael asked.

They were sitting on a rocky outcropping halfway up the ridge behind the trailers. Michael had chosen a spot high enough that their voices wouldn't carry through the clear mountain air to the occupants below.

Nicki wasn't sure why, after the way he'd acted last night, that she felt safe enough to come here alone with him. Maybe because she believed him. Both his apology and the explanation. Just as she had believed his promise to help her. Maybe that made her a fool, but she couldn't help it.

"Quarrels fires them,'' she said, "or they get tired of his harassment or tired of this place.''

She might have done the same thing, had she had anywhere to go. In spite of everything, however, she had hoped to find something on the ranch that would explain what she believed Gettys had done. Now, with the information Michael had received from his sources, she was beginning to wonder if the senator had had anything at all to do with that attack.

"Orbock didn't say anything to you about a run-in with Quarrels.''

"If he were going tell somebody, it would have been Ralph.''

She hadn't dared strike up any friendships. That had been the worst part of these long months on the Half Spur. The lack of human contact.

She acknowledged that was a large part of the reason she'd been so ready to believe what Michael told her yesterday. Ready to confide in him. Maybe it was even part of the reason she was out here tonight.

She was vulnerable to what he offered in a dozen different ways. Not the least of which had to do with her own sexuality, she admitted. Something she had been forced to deny for almost a year.

She was a woman, longing to be a woman again. And whatever else Michael Wellesley might be, he was a very attractive man. A man who also professed to want to help her. Who claimed to have the skills and the connections that would make that possible. She would have a hard time walking away from all that.

"Then he didn't mention finding any kind of lab facility to you either, I suppose?"

"Here?"

"Mapes says there's a lab on the ranch. That Orbock stumbled across it."

She shook her head. "I don't think we exchanged a dozen words. I do remember that he liked to shoot. Target practice. He'd go off on his own. On his time. Quarrels didn't like it, but he couldn't come up with a good reason for objecting. Not that something like that stops Quarrels. Anyway, I overheard him warn Orbock not to go past the substations."

"Substations? As in…power stations?"

"Utility trailers. They're stocked for emergencies. Medical supplies, blankets, water. The people assigned to the flock use them. I don't know why they call them substations. I got the idea from the conversation I overheard that they are near the boundaries of the ranch. Maybe the lab Ralph mentioned is, too, and Quarrels didn't want Orbock to get too close to it."

"Mapes said he left abruptly."

"Everybody leaves abruptly. Either Quarrels gets mad at them and throws them out or they just pack up and take off."

"Except you and Mapes."

"At his age, Ralph would have a hard time getting hired somewhere else. And I get the impression he doesn't have any resources to tide him through the times when he can't get a steady job. You'll never see Ralph buck Quarrels, no matter what he does. I've always felt sorry for him. Quarrels treats him like dirt because he's figured out that he isn't going to leave."

"Mapes said the same thing about you."

"That Quarrels can't run me off?"

"That he treats you like dirt."

For a second or two, hearing his voice, deep and quiet in the darkness, she imagined that he cared how she was treated. Then she put that notion down to more wishful thinking.

"Quarrels needs to control people. I'm used to that. After all, I survived Gettys for more than two years." The thought that followed was sudden and illuminating. "Did they say he was one of them?"

"They?"

"Your sources. Whoever told you that story. Was Gettys supposed to be one of the people I had a video of?"

She still couldn't figure how it was all connected. The ranch. Gettys. Those ridiculous allegations. The attack.

"I don't know," Michael said.

His voice had changed. Maybe it was easier to hear the nuances because she couldn't see his face. No longer filled with concern, his tone seemed cold. Because he was uncomfortable with her question? Or because…

"It isn't true," she said. "What they told you. I don't

know what was in the papers, but I wasn't involved in anything like that. I swear to you.''

For a long time there was no response.

''I've requested verification,'' he said finally.

Not exactly a rousing endorsement of her honesty, but maybe that was too much to expect. After all, they were strangers, and from what he'd said, he had a long-term relationship with whoever told him that story. It wasn't surprising that he'd take their word over hers, but that didn't keep it from hurting.

''Can you take me to those substations?''

Obviously, he didn't want to respond to her claim of innocence until he'd gotten the confirmation he'd requested.

''I've only been to one of them. Quarrels likes to keep me here to do the sampling, so I'm seldom assigned to the flock. However, when the lambs are born, everybody rotates duties. Sometimes they need a little help. A night or two some place that's warm. Extra nourishment. Assistance for the mother if something goes wrong.

''Instead of coming back and forth throughout the season, we occasionally spend a night in the substation. I can take you to the one I used. Actually it isn't that far from the pasture where we took the flock yesterday.''

Yesterday. Had those terrifying moments during which she'd believed her nemesis had found her happened only one short day ago?

''And the other one?''

She shook her head, forgetting that he couldn't see the gesture. ''I don't know. On the opposite side of the property, I guess. There's bound to be a map somewhere. Maybe in the office.''

She'd never seen it, but surely the foreman would have one somewhere, if for no other reason than to be certain about the property lines. Knowing how secretive Quarrels was, he probably wouldn't put it up for everyone to see, but he might have stashed it in that huge, old-fashioned desk or in one of the filing cabinets.

"Maybe," Michael said, seeming to dismiss her speculation about the map as unimportant. "We need to get our hands on some of the blood samples."

Since they were the ones who drew that blood, it was obvious he wasn't being literal. He wanted them in his possession.

"They're numbered. I don't know how you could take one without it being missed."

"Draw extras," he suggested. "Don't label them."

"That might work, except Quarrels watches the whole process very closely. There are just enough vials for the part of the flock that's being sampled. Sometimes we may be a couple over or a couple—"

"What is it?" he asked when she stopped abruptly.

"He keeps them in the office. He has boxes of them on one of the shelves. Syringes, too."

"Then we take some while we're looking for the map."

As she realized what he intended to do, a sense of alarm flared in her stomach.

And that's exactly why you haven't accomplished anything in the time you've been here, she chided herself. She'd been afraid to look. Afraid of getting caught. Terrified that someone would take a closer look at her face or her background.

In short, she had been a coward. She still was.

"There's no time when someone isn't there." She repeated all the arguments that had prevented her from doing what he'd just proposed. "They sleep in that building at night. The cook's inside most of the day. Quarrels works in the office when he isn't supervising. I don't see how we can just waltz in and start searching.''

''And stealing,'' he said dryly.

She didn't know whether to be relieved or annoyed that he seemed amused by her objections.

''What do *you* suggest?'' She had wanted to add some derogatory appellation to that question—something like smart-ass, maybe—but she'd refrained.

He was the one who had all this experience in clandestine operations. Or so he claimed. Let *him* worry about the ''hows'' of what he wanted to do. And then let him do it.

''There's always a risk,'' he said. ''You just have to take it.''

If she had, maybe this would all be over. She'd be back home and everything that had happened would be explained away. If she'd only had the guts to do something. This was her opportunity. Michael's presence was a huge part of that. Support. Help. Expertise.

A final chance. And this time, she was determined to take it.

Chapter Eleven

"I know this may not be what you wanted to hear, but Canton's sources don't have any doubt about Nicki Carson's involvement."

It *wasn't* what he wanted to hear. Less now than when Colleen had first told him. It had taken her long enough to get the information that he didn't doubt she had carefully vetted it before she'd passed it on.

In the past four days as he'd waited for this, he had tried to put questions about Nicki's past out of his mind, concentrating on what he had been sent to the Half Spur to do. Hoping that when he talked to his sister again, something would have changed.

"You do any independent checking?" he asked, knowing he was grasping at straws.

"She's got no criminal record, if that's what you're asking. Not even a parking ticket."

"If your sources are right about the level at which that ring operated, they would have had protection—discreet and powerful enough to keep any problems like that concealed."

"I can ask," Colleen said, sounding doubtful.

"Not your sources in the media. They wouldn't have access to the kind of information I'm talking about."

"You want some kind of *official* inquiry?"

"If the people involved in the scandal were as high-profile as you've suggested, there will already have been one."

Even rumors of a call-girl ring and blackmail in that stratosphere would have set off national security alarms. Somebody would already have looked into it, probably the FBI.

"I can try to find out," Colleen said.

"If you get stonewalled, call Landry Soames at the Bureau. Tell him I'm asking."

"Okay."

"And see what you can find on a Gene or Eugene Orbock." He spelled the last name into the satellite phone. "I'm particularly interested in his current whereabouts. And I'm going to be sending you some blood samples from the flock here. We draw new ones tomorrow. I'll drive into town on Saturday and overnight them to you. Have someone take them to the CDC in Ft. Collins."

"Any idea what they should be looking for?"

"Not a clue. There's always the possibility this is a legitimate research project. Given the dynamics of the place, I'll be surprised if that turns out to be the case. Whoever these samples are ultimately intended for, they're picked up here and transported by helicopter. That hardly sounds routine to me."

"You think there's some kind of time factor involved that would necessitate that?"

"Maybe, but that's sheer speculation. Sorry I can't get the ones I'm sending you there as quickly as that."

"I'll pass the information on to the CDC with the sample, just in case that might make a difference in the results. Anything else I need to know or do?"

"Somebody searched my trailer. I went into town last Sunday. It must have happened while I was gone."

The search had been fairly inept. A dozen small, telltale signs had been left behind. He would have known, even if the hidden traps he'd laid for just such an eventuality hadn't been sprung.

"Anything around for them to find?"

"Not where they looked." The heater where he'd concealed the phone had not been disturbed. "I'd gone up on the ridge the night before. I'd heard the chopper that picks up the samples come in and decided to investigate. The foreman had brought one of the dogs along on the exchange. The collie alerted them I was there."

She might as well know everything, he'd decided. Colleen was now his boss. She had a right to an accurate report about what he was doing.

"But they didn't see you?"

"No, but since I'm the newest hand, I'm probably the prime suspect. Maybe now that they found nothing suspicious in the trailer, they'll put the dog's barking down to some wildlife in the vicinity."

"And maybe they won't. Maybe they're planning to pay more attention to what you're doing."

"Nothing very constructive. This past week I've nosed around everything up here. And I have to tell you, I've seen nothing that seems to relate in any way to the Langworthy kidnapping."

"It was a long shot. We knew that from the first."

"Maybe, but the Gettys connection still bothers me. It seems too coincidental."

"His connection to the ranch or to Nicola Carson?"

He took a breath, determined to be in complete control before he attempted to answer that. Colleen's next question interrupted that process.

"Did you ever think that the scandal with Nicola could have been a setup?"

"Meaning what?" Even he could detect the strong thread of interest in his voice.

"Maybe the attack represented Gettys's first choice—to permanently silence Nicki in order to do away with any danger her knowledge about his connection to the ranch might represent. Whoever he sent to do that screwed up, and in the aftermath she disappeared. Gettys can't find her, so killing her is no longer an option. He turns to the next best thing. What better way to discredit anything a woman might say than to brand her a blackmailing prostitute?"

It made sense. Maybe because he wanted it to, he acknowledged, but it did.

If Gettys feared Nicki might know something dangerous about the ranch, and he hadn't succeeded in putting an end to that threat by killing her, he might very well try something else. Knowing Gettys, it could be something just that slimy.

"You find evidence of anything like that?"

"Not yet," Colleen admitted. "I haven't really had time. I was late in considering other possibilities."

"What made you decide to consider them at all?"

"Something in your voice."

He let the silence expand because he couldn't think of anything to say in response. He hadn't wanted to believe what Colleen had told him. And he knew why.

He also knew that emotion shouldn't play any part in a decision like this. Besides, where there was that much smoke, in his experience there was usually a flame or two.

"I think that until you find something concrete to support the idea of a setup," he said carefully, "we'll have to take the other information you were given into consideration."

"There is such a thing as personal judgment."

Which can always be influenced by other factors. In this case, he knew too well what those were.

"You should get the blood samples in a few days," he said, shifting the conversation back into safer territory.

"Don't do anything to acquire them that will make someone more suspicious of you," Colleen warned. "Even if this isn't related to the kidnapping, it's obvious *something's* going on there. Something they don't want made public."

That was the same conclusion he'd come to.

"The biggest danger here is slow death by boredom," he said reassuringly. "Or maybe by food poisoning."

Not exactly true, but the other threats he faced were all of the emotional sort. And they weren't something he was about to admit to his sister.

"YOU OKAY?" Michael asked, adding his efforts to those of the old man in getting the recalcitrant ewe out of the enclosure.

Ralph Mapes looked up in surprise at the question. His eyes were bloodshot and more rheumy than when he'd begged a ride into town last weekend. Despite the dryness of the mountain air, a fine dew of perspiration covered his skin, which looked sallow beneath his tan.

"Me? I'm fine. Why you asking?"

"I don't know. You seem quiet. Maybe…a little tired."

After a week on the ranch, Michael had found that the physical demands of today's sampling were far less trying than the first one had been. He and Nicki worked smoothly together, quickly falling back into the pattern they'd established last Friday.

Today Mapes had been assigned to handle the removal of the sheep from the sampling pen after the blood had been drawn—the same job Sal Johnson had handled last week. Despite Michael's help, the old man was struggling with it.

A couple of times he'd let one of the sheep he was supposed to be sending through the exit shoot back into the enclosure, endangering the contents of the table where the sampling equipment had been set up. Even after he managed a successful and relatively uneventful release, he leaned against the fence as if exhausted.

In addition, Ralph had been far less talkative than at any other time in their brief acquaintance. The difference had been marked enough to cause Nicki to raise her eyebrows in inquiry when she'd noticed Michael was watching him.

"Ain't tired. I just got work to do," Mapes said shortly. "And Charlie don't like no talking."

As he made that observation, the old man glanced toward the outer fence where the foreman was standing, beefy forearms propped on the top rail, his chin atop them. Michael's gaze followed to find Quarrels was indeed watching them.

"Not under the weather, are you?" he asked, ignoring the foreman and shifting his attention back to Mapes.

"Not enough so's I can't do my job. You just do yours and leave me alone." It was obvious the elderly cowboy not only was reluctant to talk, he resented the possibility that Michael's attempt at conversation might call him to the boss's attention.

To be fair, Quarrels *had* ridden him all afternoon. Maybe no harder than he had anyone else, but as Nicki had observed a few days ago, Mapes was probably the only one of them who couldn't afford to be sacked.

Michael walked back to the table, prepared to signal Frank Meadows, who was working the other end of the enclosure, to let in the next animal. As he passed by her, Nicki whispered to him, her head down so Quarrels couldn't see the movement of her lips, ''I think Ralph's sick.''

Maybe he was, but Michael knew the old man wouldn't appreciate interference, fearing the foreman would use any excuse he could find to fire him. Knowing Quarrels's reputation, Ralph was probably right. All either of them could do was to keep a watchful eye on the elderly cowboy.

Just as Quarrels was, Michael verified, sneaking a sideways look at the foreman while he caught and positioned the lamb that had just come through the entry shoot. Maybe if Quarrels was focusing all his attention on Mapes, however, he wouldn't be watching the rest of the operation too carefully.

He turned back to find Nicki's eyes on his face. She shook her head, the movement slight. *A warning?*

If so, it was one he didn't intend to heed. Quarrels's attention was divided because he was trying to watch both Mapes and the operation. He'd already assigned Johnson and Dawkes to take this part of the flock back up to the pasture tomorrow, leaving Michael with a dwindling number of options for acquiring the blood samples he'd promised Colleen. And none of those were good.

He could palm a couple of the vials now or he could come back down to the pens tonight when the dogs were on guard. Of course, that would only work if there were extra vials and syringes left on the table today. Or if he wanted to try to steal some from the cabin, right out from under Quarrels's nose.

Any way he did it, there was risk, but he was a risk taker. He always had been. If they ran short of vials at the end of the sampling because he'd palmed a couple, he could always claim they'd been short when they began.

He thought briefly about saying a few had been trampled in the melee after one of the animals got away from Mapes, but he quickly discarded that excuse as unacceptable. He wasn't willing to chance getting the old man sacked, not even for Colleen's investigation. Especially not if the foreman's fuse was as short as everyone claimed.

Maybe if he really believed whatever was going on here had something to do with the Langworthy baby's disappearance, it might have made a difference in that decision. He didn't.

If suspicion fell on anyone about the missing vials, it had better fall on him. After the incident with the helicopter, he was probably already on Quarrels's shortlist to watch. If he got canned, he'd simply take Nicki with him to the Royal Flush. Despite everything, he had already decided there was no way he could leave her here without his protection.

While he was reaching those decisions, thoughts ricocheting through his brain, Nicki had been preparing the syringe to take blood from the lamb. Michael glanced again at Quarrels, who was still concentrating on the old man.

"Draw two," he ordered under his breath, his eyes again lowered to the small wooly back. "Don't look up," he warned.

She didn't, but she did hesitate before she turned away from the table and toward the lamb. She bent, adroitly slipping the needle into the vein in the neck. From this angle he could see the extra vial cupped in her palm.

"He's not watching," he assured her, the words a breath, his gaze flicking back and forth between the foreman and what Nicki was doing.

The first vial was almost full. He raised his eyes to study her face. No one looking at its calm serenity would have had any hint she was up to something other than doing her job.

With a minimum of movement she changed out the vials, palming the full one and slipping the other into its place.

The dark crimson blood flowed through the syringe, filling the second one as the seconds ticked by.

When she finally turned back to the table, she was still holding both samples cupped in her hand. Michael openly focused on the table now as he waited for her to prepare the label for the sample.

While she did, he looked up and met Quarrels's eyes. They seemed intent on what the two of them were doing. The foreman still hadn't said anything, however. Surely if he knew what was going on, he would attempt to stop them.

Michael's fingers, trembling slightly with tension, found the lamb's identification tag. He read out the numbers, thankful his voice seemed steady. Using a thin-line marker, Nicki jotted them down on one white label and then another. She peeled one off the sheet and affixed it to a vial.

One vial. At least that's all he saw.

Her voice perfectly natural, as was her demeanor, Nicki nodded. "Okay."

Normally Michael would have picked the lamb up and carried it by hand over to Mapes. Instead, acting deliberately, he simply released it.

The tiny creature took off with a shake of its tail, loudly bleating its displeasure with the entire procedure. Mapes tried to catch it, but his lunge managed to frighten the animal into a U-turn. Michael moved away from the table, hoping Quarrels's eyes would follow him rather than remaining on what Nicki was doing. And hoping she would be smart enough to take advantage of the distraction he'd just arranged.

When the lamb had finally been corralled and forced through the shoot, Michael walked back to the table. He allowed his eyes to meet those of the watching foreman, careful not to convey any kind of challenge in his glance.

Quarrels's expression appeared considering, but he didn't

say anything. After a moment, he turned his head, seeming to concentrate on Frank Meadows, who was in the process of releasing the next sheep into the pen. This one was a good-sized ewe that seemed totally unconcerned about what was going to happen to her.

"Take one more," Michael instructed sotto voce as he passed Nicki.

She gave no outward sign that she'd heard him, but he had no doubt she would manage the next pilfered vial as smoothly as she had the last. And when she had, all he would have to do was get them into town and into Colleen's hands. Maybe then they'd be able to figure out some part, if only a small one, of this puzzle.

"YOU CAN'T BE SHORT," Quarrels said. "I counted them out myself."

When she'd realized she was going to run short, Nicki had planned to fake drawing blood from the last two animals, but the foreman had unexpectedly entered the enclosure while the sampling was still going on. She couldn't remember that ever happening before.

Of course, they'd been running late because of the trouble Mapes had getting the sheep into the exit shoot. The delay had exacerbated Quarrels's always uncertain temper, so that he'd been yelling at everyone during the past half hour.

His proximity had reduced the old man to trembling ineptitude, so that Michael had done most of Mapes's work as well as his own. It had also narrowed Nicki's options for hiding the glaring reality that two vials were missing.

"Maybe you miscounted—" she began.

"Like *hell*. They was all there when we started. Now they ain't. What the hell's going on?"

She shrugged. The foreman's mud-colored eyes shifted

from her face to Michael's, where they rested for several seconds. It was almost as if Quarrels were waiting for him to confess.

"I didn't count them," Michael said finally, although he hadn't been asked for an explanation. "Maybe a couple rolled off the table and got broken." He bent, pretending to look for the nonexistent vials on the ground.

"Strange that they ain't never done that before," Quarrels said sarcastically.

Michael's shrug echoed her own. It didn't pacify the foreman. The red flush in his thick neck was beginning to deepen, and veins pulsed at his temples.

"You two better find 'em or else," he threatened.

Quarrels was the classic bully. He intimidated and then fed on the fear that intimidation produced. Just as he had with Ralph today.

Nicki had always given in to his demands before because not calling attention to herself had been more important than anything he might say or do to her. Maybe if she stood up to him this time, it would be such a shock that he'd back off. That, too, would be typical of that kind of personality.

"We were short from the first," Nicki said again, working on keeping her voice deep and completely assured. "We can't find what was never here."

She had the satisfaction of watching shock invade the foreman's eyes at the boldness of the answer. Unfortunately, it didn't last long.

"What the hell makes you—"

"*I'm* the one who took them off the table," she said, looking him straight in the face. "One vial for each animal that came through. We're two short."

She was aware that she'd surprised not only Quarrels, but Michael as well. He had turned to look at her, making her wonder if he thought she was taking too great a chance. After listening to Quarrels browbeat Ralph for the last hour, standing up to him was almost worth the risk.

There was a pregnant silence. During it, she steeled herself for the foreman's anger and heard instead the distinctive thromp of a helicopter rotor.

Quarrels's gaze left her face, tracking toward the sky behind the cabin. His mouth had already opened, maybe in preparation of dressing her down. Now it widened, literally dropping, cartoonlike, as he watched the chopper's approach.

The black craft passed over their heads, flying low enough that the penned sheep milled in panic and dust swirled upward before it headed toward the ridge behind the trailers. There was nothing clandestine about this visit.

"Get this finished *now*," the foreman ordered, pivoting to maintain sight of the helicopter. He began to hurry to the gate that led out of the enclosure.

"What about the vials we're short?" she asked.

Hand on the latch, Quarrels turned back. Still looking at her speculatively, he yelled, "Mapes?"

Without any livestock to manage, the old man had been sitting on his heels, his back against the fence and his head lowered. At the sound of his name, he struggled to his feet.

"Yes, sir, boss," he called, hurrying toward the table. "What you need?"

"Go get two vials and a couple of syringes out of the office. Boxes are on the second shelf. And don't you let another animal get loose, damn it. You been slowing things down all day."

"Will do," Ralph said.

He changed directions immediately and headed across the enclosure toward the gate on the cabin side. Quarrels didn't wait to see if his order would be obeyed. He obviously had little doubt that if he said, "Jump," Mapes would ask "How high?"

The foreman slammed the gate behind him and ran toward his pickup. As soon as he climbed into the cab and closed the door behind him, Nicki turned and yelled to the old man, "I'll get the vials, Ralph. You need to take it easy."

The unexpected offer stopped Mapes in his tracks. It was almost possible to trace the conflicting thoughts in his face as he considered it. For a moment it seemed as if his fear of Quarrels might win out. Then, almost physically wilting as he made his concession, he nodded.

As Nicki walked past him, he leaned against the fence. She cast a quick glance behind her when she reached the other side of the enclosure. The pickup was disappearing up the chert road that led behind the ridge.

Whatever the significance of the helicopter, its daylight appearance outweighed the foreman's usual concerns about overseeing the sampling operation. That could only be to their advantage.

If she could get into the office and make her search without anyone seeing her, maybe they would have some place to start the investigation Michael had been sent here to conduct. Whatever the outcome, just the possibility that she might finally get her life back was worth the risk.

Chapter Twelve

It took her less than a minute to locate the boxes that held the vials and syringes. The next five she spent opening the drawers of the desk and filing cabinets and rummaging through their contents. Each racing heartbeat counted off another second of the diminishing few she could dare spend on this quest.

She expected one of the hands to enter the cabin at any minute and find her rifling through the files. She had no doubt that any of them, with the exception of Michael or Ralph, would be only too eager to tell the foreman what she'd been doing.

Frustrated by her lack of success, she closed the last of the file drawers, straightening to look around the room. Where could Quarrels have hidden the map she was convinced must exist? Her gaze fell on the only other piece of furniture in the room—the bookcase that held office supplies and a wide variety of miscellaneous items, including the vials and syringes Mapes had been sent here to retrieve.

She crossed the room, reaching high over her head to feel along the top. Her straining fingers encountered something light enough to roll away from their touch. Stretching on tiptoe and groping along the back edge, she found a long paper cylinder.

Her hand closed over it eagerly. She pulled it down, unrolling the stock as her eyes again considered the closed door. She wondered how much warning she'd have if someone were to approach. Without a porch outside the threshold, maybe none.

By the time she'd figured that out, her fingers had the paper smoothed open, revealing the map she'd been looking for. It was a standard topographical print rather than the type of map a surveyor would provide. Which meant there were no boundary marks on it, she realized in dismay.

There were penciled notations, however, mostly numbers, in a variety of places. And those could mean anything, she decided. Or nothing.

Since they were only single and double digits, it was obvious they didn't represent altitude. She concentrated on memorizing them and their relationship to the surrounding topographical features. Before she could complete the task, there was a sound from beyond the cabin door.

She released the edge of the map, letting it roll up by itself. Almost in the same motion, she threw the cylinder onto the top of the bookcase, praying it wouldn't fall back down on her head.

As the door opened behind her, the hand she'd used to pitch the map into place dropped to close over the front edge of the syringe box. She pulled it forward, tilting the whole thing toward her as if she had been studying the contents.

"Charlie know you're here?"

She half turned, looking over her shoulder without releasing the box. Sal Johnson stood in the doorway.

"We ran short of vials," she said. "He sent me to get some."

Johnson's face reflected his skepticism. "*Charlie* sent you in here?"

"I think that chopper threw him," she ventured, wondering if Johnson, who lived in the main cabin, might be more informed than the rest of them about the mission of that helicopter. If so, maybe he'd be inclined to share some of that knowledge with her. "He seemed in a big hurry to get out there and meet it."

"Charlie knows which side his bread's buttered on," Johnson said with a snigger.

Nicki debated pursuing that, but decided in this case discretion might well be the better part of valor. She didn't want to do anything that would make Johnson remember this encounter or, more dangerous, bring it to the attention of Quarrels. After all, the foreman hadn't told *her* to come here. With his own lack of compassion, he would probably question why she had offered to take Mapes's place on the errand.

"Gotta go," she said, scooping a couple of vials out of the box. She slipped them into her shirt pocket and then grabbed two syringes from the adjoining box. She turned to find Johnson still watching her.

"Something wrong?" she asked.

"Guess not," he said, moving away from the door. "Not as long as Charlie knows you're here."

Clutching the syringes, she walked across the office to the door. She opened it, aware that Johnson was following every move. She stepped through to the outside, turning slightly to pull the door shut behind her.

As she did, she made one last scan of the room. On the top of the bookcase the map lay at an angle, one end sticking out over the edge.

Not the kind of thing anyone else would notice, she comforted herself. Not unless they were looking for it.

Anyway, there was nothing she could do about it now.

She closed the door behind her and began to run across the compound toward the enclosure.

"HERE. AND THEN HERE," Nicki said, writing numbers on the map she'd sketched. "This one corresponds fairly closely to the location of the substation I told you about. I'm not sure I've ever been to the other."

"So it *could* be the second substation," Michael said, thinking out loud.

"Or something else," she said. "Anything else, actually."

She had looked up at his question, her eyes dark and wide in the low light of his trailer. The generator had been shut down for the night, so the only illumination was her small penlight.

Michael had held it while Nicki tried to recreate the map she'd seen this afternoon in the office. Since she was far more familiar with the property than he was, he was dependent on both her memory of the markings she'd seen, as well as her interpretation of them.

"Why don't we go see what it is," he suggested.

"Tomorrow?"

They had been assigned to check fence in the southeastern quadrant of the ranch. It wasn't as if Quarrels or anyone else would know whether or not they'd done that.

All they had to do was ride out of the compound in the proper direction. As soon as they were far enough away from the ranch, they could double back toward the location Nicki had just marked on the sketch.

Michael wasn't comfortable with Johnson having seen her in the office this afternoon. She had managed to hide her identity this long because she'd been careful to do nothing that would draw attention to herself. Now she had.

He also didn't like the reappearance of the helicopter.

Not when there were no blood samples ready to be picked up. Not when the craft appeared so openly over the compound, something Nicki had verified had never happened before. And he especially hadn't liked Quarrels's reaction to it.

All those things indicated that something on the Half Spur had suddenly changed. In an investigation like this, where they were pretty much stumbling around in the dark, change was not a good thing.

"The sooner, the better," he said.

He had no doubt his instinct was right. The sooner he wrapped this up and got Nicki out of here, the better it would be for her.

He'd survived this long by never ignoring what his gut told him. The interior warning this time was as clear and unequivocal as any he'd ever had. The only difference was that the premonition of danger centered around Nicki. He understood why that was so, even if he hadn't yet admitted it to himself.

If he screwed up, she was the one who would pay the price. And that was something he couldn't afford.

"I'm not sure about the numbers," she said, lowering her gaze to the drawing again. The pen she held hovered above the paper a few seconds until she made a tentative mark near the highest part of the terrain that surrounded the ranch.

"Maybe…here," she said finally. It seemed almost a question.

The spot she'd marked was a more likely location for the lab Mapes had told him about, he thought. Isolated and remote, there would be little danger of someone from the ranch stumbling onto it by accident.

Not unless they had done exactly what Orbock had done

and gone wandering around by themselves. Something Quarrels tried his damnedest to prevent.

"I think we ought to check there first," he said.

"I'm less sure about this location," she warned. "Johnson interrupted me before I could commit everything to memory. This is an estimate at best."

Again her eyes lifted from the map to meet his.

"It's more than we had yesterday."

She nodded, seeming reluctant to take credit for how far she'd advanced their cause. As frightened as she must have been by the attack in Washington, it had taken real courage to do what she'd done this afternoon. It was past time for him to acknowledge that.

"Thanks for what you did today. It took guts."

She shook her head, her brow wrinkling slightly as if she had no idea what he was talking about.

"Searching the office."

The furrows cleared, but she shook her head again.

"I should have done it months ago. I told myself I'd come here to figure this all out. How Gettys and the attack were connected to this place. Instead, I just hid. I crawled into this rat hole and pulled it in over my head."

"There's nothing wrong with taking cover when you're under attack."

"But there *is* something wrong with never coming out again."

"You have now. Just don't start feeling too brave. Whether or not what's going on here is connected to Gettys or to Washington, someone seems to have taken pains to make sure it remains undercover. We can't know to what lengths they'll go to keep it hidden."

She nodded, but he wasn't convinced she had bought into his concern. After months of being too frightened to make a move, she had obviously found action exhilarating. That heady sense of again being in charge of her own destiny could be addictive. And dangerous.

"We'll start there in the morning," he said, pointing to the location she'd called an estimate. It made sense to him that whatever they were most determined to hide would be as far removed from the main compound as they could manage, and this was. "We find nothing there, we'll try the other locations."

She nodded, flicking off the miniature flashlight. They stood together, unmoving in the sudden darkness.

Maybe she was waiting for her eyes to adjust. Or maybe, as he was, she was thinking about the last time she'd come here.

Once more he could smell the soap she'd used during her shower. There was nothing feminine about the scent, except that it was associated in his mind with the night he'd kissed her. Trying to punish her for not being what he'd thought she was. Now both the fragrance and the darkness evoked the memory of her body trembling in his arms.

She turned to head toward the door, and he realized that, despite everything, he didn't want her to go. The courage that had prompted her to take Mapes's place today was what had attracted him from the first.

From the moment Nicki had pulled that knife on him, defending herself against a man she believed had come to kill her, he had been interested. A strange aphrodisiac, perhaps, but one that, given his background, was probably inevitable.

As soon as she'd moved, his fingers had closed over her forearm. As he stopped her forward motion, he sensed rather than saw that she'd turned back to face him.

"What is it?"

He said nothing of what he'd been thinking. He exerted pressure on her arm instead, urging her to him.

Surprisingly, there was no resistance. She stepped into his arms as if there had been no conflict between them.

Despite the darkness, his mouth found hers, unerringly fastening over her lips as if by right of possession. Her response was immediate. Her hand lifted to the back of his head, her fingers threading through his hair.

It was not a reaction he had any right to expect. Not after what had happened the last time she'd come here.

He had touched her then in a fury that was almost despair. Neither of those was the emotion that tightened his groin tonight, creating an aching hardness that deepened as she turned within his arms, fitting her body more closely to his.

The incredible trust that response required, especially after what he'd done, created a knot at the back of his throat. And a determination that this time would be different.

He'd seen no proof that Nicki Carson was anything other than what she claimed to be. There had been no evidence in any of her actions that she was the kind of woman who would be involved in a call-girl ring. Colleen was right. The media stories could have been fabricated to discredit anything she might say about the senator.

As he reasoned his way to that conclusion, his fingers were already busy with the top button of the shirt she wore. When they'd succeeded, he began to press kisses along the satin-smooth column of her throat, his lips trailing downward into the opening his hand created.

There was no undershirt tonight. After her shower she had apparently pulled a clean shirt over her head in order to make the short journey to his trailer. As his fingers forced the last button through its hole, the front of the garment parted, exposing her nude body to his touch.

His hands cupped under the small, perfect globes of her breasts. He lowered his head, putting his mouth against the faint heartbeat between them. The texture of the fragile skin seemed sweetly, infinitely familiar, as if he'd kissed her there a thousand times.

His lips encountered a fine chain, lying within the valley between her breasts. The fingers of his right hand traced its delicate links to the heart-shaped locket they bore.

His first reaction was anxiety. Wearing the ornament seemed risky, given her disguise. If anyone saw it—

Even as the thought formed, he realized the ridiculousness of that particular concern. In order for anyone to see the chain, they would have to do exactly what he had done. They would have to undress her. If they did, then the chain and locket would not be the most revealing evidence of her femininity.

Releasing that worry, he turned his head, deliberately allowing his late-night whiskers to graze the skin of her breast. His lips found her nipple, provoking a quick inhalation.

He ran his tongue around and then over the nub, which tightened in response. He rimmed it with moisture once more before he raised his head to blow over the dampness he'd left on her skin. She shivered in response, her hands clutching his shoulders.

Her breathing faltered again as his mouth closed over the tip of her breast, suckling strongly. Suddenly she leaned into his touch, as if her knees had given way, and whispered a single syllable into the darkness.

"Yes."

A permission which had already been given, in ways that required no verbal expression. That initial movement into his arms as if she knew she belonged there. Her fingers gripping his shoulders, short nails pressing so hard into bone and muscle that he was aware of them even through the fabric of his shirt. The shuddering breathing that mirrored every caress of his tongue.

It wasn't enough. It couldn't be. Not with the physical barriers that remained between them.

He wanted the hair-roughened, sweat-dampened skin of his chest moving over her breasts. The long, smooth muscles of her thighs lifting to meet his downward stroke. The soft sounds she made growing into breathless climax as their bodies exploded together. He wanted it all. Everything that soft "yes" had promised.

Straightening, he fumbled for the metal buttons at the front of her jeans. As he did, her fingers began to work at the ones on the chamois shirt he wore.

Too many clothes, he thought. *Too long to remove them. Too long. Too long.*

Impatiently, he stopped what he was doing and reached over his shoulder, grabbing a fistful of material and jerking his shirt off over his head. The white T-shirt came with it, despite the fact that both had been tucked into the waistband of his jeans.

When the night air touched his bare chest, the sensation reminded him of what he'd just imagined. The cool smoothness of her skin moving against the heat of his.

He closed the distance that separated them by pulling her into his embrace. For a fraction of a second, her body stiffened before the softness of her breasts collided with his chest.

He closed his eyes, fighting for control. "Too long" echoed in his consciousness, the connotation subtly different this time. *Too long without a woman. Too long alone. Too long without this.*

So long that his very skin seemed sensitized. At every point where their bodies made contact, nerve endings, feeling raw and exposed, reacted to the slightest stimuli. The tightening of her nipples. The breath she drew. The slight arching of her back to bring her lower body into contact with his. Her recoil at the unmistakable evidence of his arousal and then the subtle relaxation of her acceptance.

Acceptance. Of him. Of what he wanted.

And that was the very least of what she was entitled to from him. *Acceptance.*

His hands returned to the task they'd deserted. As they again struggled with the metal buttons, he lowered his head, his mouth seeking hers. Their tongues touched. Joined. Released.

The last of the buttons finally came free. His fingers had found already either side of the waistband of her jeans, when she whispered another word.

"Boots."

For a heartbeat, it made no sense. Not until he realized, as she obviously had, that there was no point in attempting to strip off her jeans while she was wearing her boots. Not unless he intended to take her like that.

The phrase reverberated in his head. *Take her...*

That's exactly what he had intended, he realized. To take her. To use her body to ease the aching hunger of his.

Why not? his conscience jeered at the resultant surge of guilt. *You certainly won't be the first.*

The kind of thinking that had destroyed things before. The hated images of what they'd said about Nicola Carson flickered at the edges of his consciousness, no matter how much he tried to deny them.

He had never before had a problem with a woman's past. She had as much right to take lovers as a man did. That's what he had always professed to believe, so why did the questions his sister had raised about Nicki's past bother him so damn much?

Because there's a difference in making love to a man

because you want to and in doing it for money. There was no way he could romanticize prostitution. He had seen it in some of its cruelest guises around the globe. Just because it occurred at the Mayfair or the Ritz didn't change its essential ugliness.

Perhaps Nicki sensed, and didn't yet understand, his mental withdrawal. Or maybe she believed he hesitated because of the warning she'd just given.

In any case, she caught his hand, bringing it to her lips. She pressed a kiss into the palm, and then stepped away from him.

Standing alone in the darkness, he listened to the noises as she removed first one boot and then the other, dropping them on the floor of the trailer where they landed with small, distinct thuds. He didn't move as he identified the rustling noises that signified the removal of her jeans and her shirt.

And then he didn't dare to move at all.

Still struggling for control, he was unprepared when she stepped back into his arms. Her palms rested against his chest, fingertips lying over his collarbone.

He reached up and wrapped his hands around her wrists, pulling them out to the sides. At the same time, he moved forward so that their bodies were again in contact.

The knowledge that she was completely nude intensified every sensation. The tips of her breasts brushed against the hair on his chest. His hands found the rounded curve of her bottom, decidedly feminine, despite her slimness.

He lifted, again bringing her against his arousal. Her fingers found the waistband of his jeans, working frantically at their fastening. After a moment she had the zipper undone. Her hands pushed into the opening, forcing the fabric apart.

He put his head back, eyes closing at her first touch. Heat

roared through his body as her hands freed him from the now painful constriction of his clothing.

And then, as they began to caress him, the resultant rush of blood strengthened an erection that seemed more powerful than any he'd ever felt before. His long need could explain that, of course. *Or her expertise.*

With that thought, his hand closed over hers, stopping the motion she'd begun. "Don't," he ordered softly.

And hated himself.

He could hear nothing but the blood drumming through his ears. Neither of them seemed to be breathing. The stillness grew, stretching tensely between them as he continued to hold her hand.

Finally, she twisted her wrist, attempting to pull it from his grasp. He let her go, and she took a step backward.

The distance that opened between them was less than a foot, but it was breathing room. He took a breath into it, feeling deserted, even though he had been the one who had put a stop to what had been happening. And he still wasn't sure why he had.

"Is this some kind of game?"

Considering what he'd done, her voice sounded incredibly controlled. Logical. Interested even.

"I'm sorry," he said.

He was. Sorry he'd touched her in the first place. Sorry that he was too stupid to take what she was offering. More sorry than he could possibly express that he couldn't get the image of her professionally servicing some fat-assed congressman in the exact same way she'd been touching him out of his head.

What the hell did that matter? he raged internally. She was a woman who was willing, and he was a man who—

He took another breath, trying to decide exactly what he

was right now. Given the unusual flood of emotion, it wasn't as easy as it should have been.

"I asked you a question," she said.

He ignored her, concentrating instead on deciding who he was and what he wanted.

A woman? If so, he'd just blown it.

This particular woman? If so, why the hell hadn't he taken what she was obviously offering?

Or did he want some preconceived idea of who and what he needed Nicki Carson to be? And if she wasn't that...

"I made a mistake," he said. "I had promised you this wouldn't happen again."

There was a long beat of silence.

"I didn't think this was the same," she said softly.

It hadn't been. For a multitude of reasons, including her reaction.

And yet, at the heart it *was* the same. He wanted her, but only if she wasn't what they said she was.

Even as he admitted that, he couldn't reconcile what he felt with who he was. It made no rational sense, not even to him.

"There's too much going on for this to be a good idea," he said, offering excuses. "It's too dangerous."

He was glad it was dark. That way he didn't have to look her in the eye as he mouthed that lie.

"Because this is a distraction."

"It could be."

"And you don't want that." The inflection was flat.

"I don't think a distraction is good for either one of us right now."

"Did you decide that before or after you unbuttoned my shirt?"

"This was a mistake," he said evenly. "I told you I'm sorry."

"You told me that before."

"I was sorry before."

"Am I seeing a pattern in this? Make a move and then retreat. Say you're sorry. Promise it won't happen again. If a woman does that, she gets called some very ugly names."

He said nothing in his defense. What he had done was indefensible. And he couldn't bring himself to tell her the truth: *I want you until I remember what you are.*

"It won't happen again," he said. Each word deliberate. Measured.

"You're so right," she said, laughing a little, despite the fact that her voice had trembled. "You know what they say. Fool me once…"

She didn't bother to finish the adage. Instead, she bent and retrieved her clothing from the floor. He listened as she pulled on her jeans and shirt, every motion abrupt with anger. Instead of taking time to put on her boots, she picked them up and took the two steps that separated her from the door.

As she opened it, he tried to think of something to say. Something that could make this better. And then he realized there was nothing he *could* say.

Nothing had changed. Nothing would change until he knew, beyond a shadow of doubt, the truth about Nicki Carson.

His long years in intelligence had taught him two things. To trust no one. And that the really expert liars are the ones you can never in a million years imagine are lying.

Chapter Thirteen

He had expected there would be strain between them and had been prepared to deal with it. What he hadn't expected was how bad he would feel when he looked into her eyes. Rimmed with red, they were both haunted and exhausted. And they refused to hold on his.

He couldn't tell if that was the product of anger or something else. Something he would have a much harder time dealing with, he had decided, as they'd saddled their horses side-by-side in the thin morning sunlight streaming into the barn.

There had been no opportunity for private conversation, even if they'd been inclined to talk about what had happened last night. Several of the others, including the two hands assigned to take the newly sampled flock to pasture, had also been there.

He had watched surreptitiously as Nicki got her mount and her gear ready for the day. Her motions had been quick and controlled. Unrevealing.

As she worked, she had kept her head down, a precaution she'd employed in the past. In this case he felt the gesture was directed at hiding her face not from the others, but from him.

Once mounted, she had led the way out of the compound,

riding up into a mist that was almost ghostly in the dawn light. Without discussion, but also without any attempt to back out of their plan, a move he'd been anticipating, she had then done exactly what he'd told her to do last night. She'd ridden out in the direction of their assigned work area before she doubled back, heading toward the remote peak she'd marked on the map.

Whatever else Nicki Carson might be, she was apparently a woman of her word. Despite what had happened between them last night.

He was sorry for that. Especially sorry for hurting her.

He no longer bothered to deny, at least not to himself, the strong sexual attraction he felt for her. Every time he allowed himself to get close, however, the images engendered by what Colleen had told him would be in his head. And no matter how hard he tried, he couldn't seem to banish them.

It was only when they reached that wilderness location that he realized the daunting prospect they faced in trying to pinpoint anything hidden up here. If the lab existed, however, he had already decided it would be in the highest, most rugged terrain surrounding the ranch. Needle in a haystack or not, this was where they needed to be looking.

After a couple of hours of picking their way up the mountain, they had to leave the horses to climb the increasingly steep and hostile incline on foot. Almost two hours after they'd staked their mounts, they were rapidly approaching the point of no return. If they didn't turn around soon, despite having found nothing vaguely resembling a lab, they wouldn't make it back to the compound for dinner. That was necessary to avoid any further suspicion from Quarrels or Johnson.

As much as he hated to admit defeat, especially since there was no guarantee they would be assigned to work together tomorrow, not on a job that gave them so much freedom, Michael turned to Nicki and motioned her to start back down. She met his eyes this time, holding them long enough to make a sharply negative movement of her head. Then she pointed to the top of the ridge they were climbing.

His eyes tracked upward as he tried to estimate how long it would take to reach that vantage point. By the time he had, she had scrambled past him, climbing, despite their long effort, with a determination that was almost palpable.

He had understood yesterday that this search had become some kind of crusade for her. Maybe because, as she'd said, she was ashamed of not having done this kind of investigation before. Maybe because she wanted to prove something to him, although he wasn't clear what that might be.

All he knew was that he wasn't going to let her go on alone. He gritted his teeth against the burn in his knee, which seemed to have stiffened during the few minutes of inactivity, and followed her, moving far more slowly than she was.

When he finally arrived at the top, Nicki was lying on her stomach looking over the edge. She turned her head as he eased down beside her. His breathing was ragged, loud enough to be audible in the thin mountain air.

For the first time, she met his eyes squarely. Hers were filled with what appeared to be triumph.

"Look," she said, tilting her chin toward the rim.

Across the canyon, slightly below their elevation, a series of low, rectangular buildings spread out along the side of the opposite peak. Although the terrain around the structures was as craggy as that they'd just struggled up, a smoothly graded, unpaved road led up the mountainside, giving relatively easy access to them. Two vehicles, both designed for off-road travel, were parked in tandem in front of the first of the structures.

Michael wondered briefly how they'd managed to get the materials and the manpower up here to create this place, but the construction was simple and strictly utilitarian. Built of concrete and glass blocks, both durable and relatively easy to work with, the project wouldn't have taken skilled labor. Not the exterior, at any rate. As for whatever was inside—

Nicki grabbed his forearm, her fingers digging into muscle. He turned his head, but she was no longer looking at him. As his eyes followed the focus of hers, he realized what she'd been trying to tell him.

A man, wearing a white lab coat, was walking away from the far end of the buildings. He carried a metal pump sprayer, the kind gardeners use to eradicate weeds. Michael couldn't tell if he had exited from a door at the end of the last structure or if he had come from somewhere around the back.

He approached a pen, which held a dozen or so sheep. Michael hadn't noticed it before because it was at the extreme end of the ledge the lab occupied, tucked under an overhang.

When the man reached the enclosure, he put the pump on the ground and pulled the handle up and down a couple of times to prime it. Before he picked it up again, he lifted the clear plastic mask hanging around his neck and placed it over his nose and mouth. He took time to adjust and then to check the fit before he picked up the canister again.

"What *is* that?" Nicki breathed.

Unconsciously, Michael shook his head, his eyes never leaving the man in the lab coat. He now had the sprayer under his arm, holding the nozzle out over the animals with his left hand as he moved the handle up and down with his right. Although they couldn't see what he was spraying, it seemed obvious from the nonreaction of the sheep that it was an aerosol rather than a liquid.

"Some kind of pest control?" Nicki whispered.

"Maybe," Michael conceded, although he'd never seen that method of delivery. "They do that on the Spur?" He turned in time to see her shake her head.

"I don't like it," she said softly, still focused on the opposite ridge. "I don't like this whole setup."

"We need to get closer."

She pulled her gaze away from the man in the lab coat, whom she'd been watching in almost fascinated horror. "Why?"

"We need a sample of whatever that is."

"And just how do you propose to get that?"

"Whatever that is, the wool will have absorbed it. There will be traces."

"You're planning to traipse over there and shear a sheep or two?"

The unpaved road that ran in front of the buildings didn't provide much cover. Even if he could discover where it began, it would probably be guarded. Or monitored.

If he rejected the road, that left climbing up on foot. After the trek they'd made this morning, he doubted he'd be in shape to tackle another climb anytime soon.

"You have another suggestion?" he asked. It wasn't a rhetorical question. At this point, he would welcome another viable alternative.

"Go back to whoever the hell you're working for and tell *them* about this place. Let them send somebody out here to check it out. Like maybe the Air Force."

Given Colleen's connections, he probably could at that, he thought, amused by the thought of a couple of F-16's buzzing the lab. And then he realized there would already be satellite photos of this place. By pulling the right strings, those could be acquired from the agency. Given the sophistication of their technology, they would provide details of the site he couldn't see from here.

Neither the satellites nor the Air Force, however, would be able to get a sample of whatever the guy in the white coat had just sprayed on the sheep. To do that somebody was going to have to visit that lab in person.

"Could you find the start of that road?" he asked, still examining his options.

"From the base of the compound?"

He nodded, his eyes still focused on the scientist who was returning to the building, pump sprayer in hand. As far as Michael could tell, the sheep, back to their normal placidity, were none the worse for the experience.

"Probably."

Her tone was grudging, but he didn't believe she would have agreed if she hadn't been certain she could.

"Then the next climb we make will be by pickup."

HE GLANCED AGAIN at his watch, directing the penlight Nicki had left in his trailer last night toward the dial and then clicking it off. She was more than ten minutes late.

Maybe she'd overslept. Or maybe there was someone wandering around outside, and she'd decided to lie low for a while. That was a decision he normally wouldn't argue with, but for some reason he had the feeling that things were coming to a head on the Half Spur. Tonight might be their last chance to get to that lab.

He couldn't put his finger on why he had such a heightened sense of anxiety. The visit of the helicopter, maybe. The sidelong glances from Quarrels that he'd caught out of the corner of his eye at dinner tonight. A tenseness in the atmosphere.

He flicked on the light once more, directing its narrow

beam at the face of his watch. Another two minutes had dragged by since the last time he'd looked.

He leaned closer to the outer door he'd been waiting beside, putting his ear against its thin metal skin. There was absolute silence outside. Giving up any pretense at patience, he turned the handle, exerting a slight upward pressure to try and prevent the telltale metallic squeal.

As soon as the door opened, the unmistakable smell of smoke rushed into the trailer. No longer worried about noise, he stepped down to the ground, his eyes searching for the source.

There was an eerie red glow in the direction of Mapes's trailer. Although there were woods between, it seemed clear that's where the fire must be. And he could hear it now, licking through the trees that surrounded the semicircle of trailers.

By that time, he was already running. Mapes's trailer was nearest, and next in line was Nicki's, with the thicket of aspens he'd hidden in frighteningly close behind it.

The nearer he got to the old man's trailer, the thicker the air grew. Eyes stinging, he peered through the darkness, but the pall of smoke and the glow from the fire gave a strangely distorted image of what lay ahead.

As he topped the rise that separated his trailer from Mapes's, he could see that the old man's was engulfed in flame. At least the far end was. And if it was set up like his own—

The explosion rocked the eerie quiet of the night. As he'd feared, the propane tank on the trailer had been in the same location as on his. The resulting shock wave literally caused him to stumble backward. Righting himself, he hesitated a moment, shielding his eyes with his hand as debris rained down around him.

The fire seemed to gain new life from the blast. It had

begun to devour everything in its path with a great whoosh-ing sound.

Whatever thoughts he'd had about getting Mapes out seemed doomed as he watched the flames race from the end of the trailer that had already been involved to the other. If the old man was in there, it was too late to help him.

Michael lifted his eyes, for the first time looking beyond the inferno of the burning trailer. Fueled by the explosion, the fire was roaring through the trees on the far side. And the next trailer—

He was running again, heat and the smoke all around him. As he approached the blazing shell of Mapes's former home, a figure appeared out of the smoke, silhouetted against the red glow behind it.

Someone come to help? Or, please God, could it be Nicki?

Fear sent adrenaline through his bloodstream. He wasn't even aware of the pain in his damaged knee.

As he neared the figure, he knew from size alone it couldn't be Nicki. Too short and too thick.

"Who's there?" he called without slowing his stride.

"Mapes," the old man said. "Oh, my God. Oh, my God."

"You okay?"

Reluctantly Michael slowed. He was near enough now that, with the light from the fire, he could see the cowboy's face. Eyes wide, Mapes was staring at the burning trailer as if he couldn't believe what was happening. He nodded in response to Michael's question without turning to look at him.

"I woke up, and it was on fire. Never thought about the tank blowing, but I knew I had to get out of there."

Almost a miracle, Michael thought, because otherwise…

"Go down to the main cabin," he shouted, taking Mapes's arm and trying to get through to him. "Get the others. Bring them up to the next trailer. Beaumont's trailer. We've got to put it out or it will burn them all."

"Nate." Mapes turned his head and looked toward the fire that was sweeping through the trees. "You got to get the kid," he said, almost as if he'd just realized the danger.

"I will. Go get us some help."

Without waiting to see if he'd been obeyed, Michael started his awkward run again. The fire was moving through the dry woods far faster than he would have believed possible, heading straight for Nicki.

He had to skirt around the path it took. He was panting, his eyes, nose and throat raw from the acrid air he was trying to breathe. And he cursed the damaged leg that made it seem as if he were running through quicksand, although he was pushing himself to the limit.

He angled up the slope, cutting through the trees, desperate for his first glimpse of Nicki's trailer. When he did, his worse fears were realized. The flames had traveled faster than he had.

Maybe she had already gotten out. Maybe, like Mapes, she had awakened in time. Maybe the tank's explosion had given her warning.

Please, God, he prayed, toiling through air that felt too dense to pull into his straining lungs. *Please God, let her be out.*

And then he was there. Despite the intensity of the heat, he stepped up on the single wooden step and pulled at the handle of the door.

It wouldn't turn. He tried for maybe three seconds, putting the full weight of his body into the effort. Nothing.

It seemed to be locked. Which meant Nicki was still

inside. He pounded on the metal with his fist, still trying to force the handle downward.

"Nicki? Wake up, Nicki. Open the door, damn it."

There was no response. Although only the end nearest Mapes's trailer was in flames, the smoke inside was probably enough that she might have been overcome, lying unconscious as the fire ate its way in.

He had to get her out. He rammed his shoulder against the door. Although the wooden step proved a poor platform from which to launch that kind of attack, he hit the door again and then again, feeling it shudder under the force of the blows.

Still, it didn't give. It was hard to conceive that something so flimsy could withstand his assault, but it was.

Giving up, he backed off the step, looking at the narrow windows. He might break through them, but he couldn't get in and Nicki couldn't get out. And opening them would only provide more oxygen to fuel the combustion.

Frantic now, he looked for something to use as a battering ram. Maybe the propane tank off the back. As soon as he thought of it, he realized the potential for disaster. He even thought about going back for the truck and ramming it into the side of the trailer. There was no time for that, of course. No time for anything he could think of. No time.

He *had* to force the door. It was his only chance. Having reached that decision, he climbed back onto the wooden step, pushing the handle down with both hands.

"Nicki! Answer me, damn it. Wake up, Nicki!"

There was no response. Once more he began slamming his shoulder against the door. It shook under the ferocity of his blows, but refused to open.

He tried to move back a little to gather momentum. The wooden step teetered under the uneven distribution of his weight so that he was forced to jump off. It turned over as he did. Only then did he realize that the step, shaped like a small bench, wasn't attached to the frame of the trailer.

He picked it up and used it like a battering ram, banging it again and again against the door. The resultant metallic clangs would surely bring help, even if the door continued to withstand the assault.

More in fury and frustration than with any conscious plan, he lifted the bench and brought the end of it down at an angle, striking the handle. There was a popping noise that didn't seem to be related to the approaching fire.

Encouraged, he raised the bench to the full extent of his reach before he slammed it again into the metal door. It gave unexpectedly, and both Michael and the bench fell into the choking smoke inside Nicki's trailer.

Chapter Fourteen

The acrid cloud that thickened the air outside was a hundred times worse here. Because the door had opened so suddenly, Michael hadn't had a chance to grab a lungful of it before he found himself in the airless hell of the trailer.

There was no time to worry about it now. Every second counted, and too many of them had passed as he'd pounded on the door. He had to locate Nicki and then get her out of here. With zero visibility and without any point of reference other than the interior of his own trailer.

He could only hope hers was set up the same. He felt his way back to the area analogous to that where his bunk was located. Maybe she'd never awakened, despite the explosion. Maybe she'd been overcome by smoke in her sleep.

If she had, he realized, panic clenching his gut, it might already be too late. He deliberately pushed the possibility that Nicki could be dead out of his mind as his hands frantically searched the mattress he'd finally located.

The bunk was empty. And there was no way to explore this end of the trailer further. The flames were already here, their heat searing his exposed face and hands relentlessly.

As he made his way back to the exit, he tried to make sure he wasn't missing her. Since he couldn't see a foot in front of his face, she could be lying unconscious anywhere along the way.

Lungs aching, he finally reached the open door. The lesser darkness outside provided some illumination, now that his eyes had adjusted to the pitch-black of the smoke-filled interior. On the floor, just on the other side of the opening, lay a crumpled shape.

Nicki. Just let her be alive.

He could tell from both the sound and the sudden flare of light from behind him that the fire had reached the bunk he'd just left. It picked up intensity as it fed on the highly flammable bedding. In a matter of seconds it would have consumed everything there, its insatiable red maw searching for something new to devour.

As he bent over Nicki, he realized he would have a hard time picking her up and carrying her out. Although she was thin, she was tall, especially for a woman, and the solid muscle she had built in the months on the Half Spur would be dead weight. The quickest way to get her out into the fresh air would be to drag her through the open doorway. He stooped behind her head and gripped her under the arms.

By now the lack of oxygen was beginning to affect him. Light-headed, he strained to turn her limp body and pull her out. He cushioned her descent as well as he could as he dragged her down the steps and away from the burning trailer.

Only when he'd gone far enough that the air didn't sear his lungs did he dare stop. He bent over Nicki, who was still motionless. He put the first two fingers of his right hand against the artery in her neck. Beneath them, faintly, he could feel the pulse of blood.

The glow from the fire behind him lit her still features. She looked as if she were sleeping. *Please, God,* he prayed again as he tilted her head back, opening the airway, and started CPR.

While he worked, he was aware that people were arriving on the scene, some on foot and some in vehicles. Ignoring them, he continued the procedures, clearing everything but their precise rhythms from his mind.

It seemed an eternity before he felt the first movement beneath his lips. Nicki tried to cough and gagged instead.

He raised his head, watching her. The instinctive effort to draw in air resulted in a coughing jag. He waited it out, knowing this was a necessary part of the process of clearing the smoke from her lungs.

Although he had lifted his mouth away from hers, he didn't move more than a few inches until he was sure she was breathing on her own. When he was finally satisfied of that, he slipped his arm under her shoulders and helped her sit up.

Another explosion rent the night. He hunched his back, turning it toward the burning trailer and using his body to shield Nicki's from the falling debris.

Her hand came up, trembling, to touch his cheek. By the light of the fire, he could read the question in her eyes.

"It's okay," he said. "You're outside. Everything's going to be all right."

"Wouldn't open," she whispered.

The effort at speech produced another coughing spell. This one was prolonged enough that, as he waited it out, still supporting her shoulders, Michael turned his head to check on the progress of the fire.

Someone had organized a shovel brigade. Silhouetted against the blaze, the dark shapes of the Half Spur's employees toiled to throw dirt on the flames.

And it appeared they were winning the battle. If they could keep the blaze confined to the relatively clear area beyond Nicki's trailer, they had a chance of stopping it before it could cause any further destruction.

"Jammed," Nicki whispered, her voice hoarse with the effects of the smoke she'd inhaled. "From the outside."

Michael turned back at the words, realizing their implication. In the crimsoned reflection from the flame, her eyes were wide and very dark as they looked up into his.

"Are you saying…you think someone *tried to trap* you inside?"

She nodded, her eyes tracking to the trailer, now completely embroiled in flame.

"Are you sure that—"

"I'm sure the door wouldn't open. The lock was jammed somehow."

A chill of horror edged along his spine. To set a fire in these conditions was bad enough. As insane as someone would have to be to do that, it was a thousand times worse to deliberately imprison someone inside to face a death that didn't bear thinking about. The vilest kind of murder.

"Is he okay?"

Michael turned to find Charlie Quarrels at his elbow. Hands on his knees, the foreman bent forward, peering down at Nicki. The shapeless tee and drawstring pajama pants she wore hid her femininity as thoroughly as her daytime attire.

"Somebody jammed the lock on Nate's trailer," Michael said.

The time for games was done. There was no way he was going to leave Nicki here, not another hour. Whatever else was happening on the Half Spur, the Langworthy baby wasn't here. He doubted any of this was related to the kidnapping. They had the blood samples and the location of the lab. All that was left was to get Nicki out of here before something else happened.

"Whadda you mean 'jammed the lock'?" Quarrels repeated in what sounded like genuine confusion.

"I couldn't get it open," Nicki said.

"That don't mean somebody *jammed* it. Heat makes metal swell. Probably got stuck. Why the hell would somebody want to lock you in, boy? That's pure crazy."

The expanding metal explanation was just plausible enough that it held both of them silent for a moment.

"The same reason they'd want to set a fire in the first place," Michael said.

"You can blame that old fool for that," Quarrels said.

Old fool? "Mapes?"

"I told him a thousand times. No smoking inside the quarters. He does it anyway. I warned him something like this was gonna happen."

Again, the explanation made sense. They were all aware of the depths of Ralph's addiction. Besides, the old man hadn't felt well for the past couple of days. It was possible he had disobeyed the foreman's injunction. More than possible, Michael admitted, remembering the smoke he'd smelled as he'd waited outside Nicki's trailer.

"Looks like they got it under control," Quarrels said.

Michael glanced over his shoulder. The fire had totally gutted Nicki's trailer and was still smoldering in the woods behind it, but it no longer raced along the ground or leaped from treetop to treetop.

"I'm taking the kid into Granby," Michael said, putting his hand under Nicki's elbow. Despite his encouragement, she made no attempt to get up.

"What for?" Quarrels demanded. "He's okay. Ain't you, boy?"

Nicki nodded, her eyes on Michael's face.

"He's suffering from smoke inhalation," he said. "He

needs to be checked out by someone who knows what they're doing.''

"Looks okay to me," Sal Johnson said. The cowboy was standing behind Quarrels, looking down at Nicki.

"Not exactly what I'd call a professional opinion," Michael said.

"He just needs to get up and walk around," Johnson said. "I think we got it, boss."

"Make sure," Quarrels said. "Thinking won't cut it. And somebody's gonna have to stay up here tonight and make sure it don't flare up. How about it, McAdams? Seems like you're the logical candidate."

"I told you. I'm taking Nate into town. He needs to be checked out."

"And I told you there ain't no need for that. You keep an eye out up here. I'll take the kid and Ralph down to the cabin. There's a couple of cots we can set up for them for tonight."

Like hell, Michael thought. Now that he thought about it, Ralph might have been another intended victim.

The motivation behind that was less clear, however. Maybe the old man had let slip to one of the other hands that he knew about the lab. Or, even more dangerous, that he'd told Michael. If that were the case, none of them could afford to spend another night on the Spur.

"Get somebody else," he said, again urging Nicki to rise.

This time, with his help, she managed to struggle to her feet. The effort provoked another fit of coughing. If nothing else, that would have convinced him that he'd made the right decision in taking her to the emergency room.

"I'm giving you an order," Quarrels said, his voice hard.

"And I'm refusing it. Get somebody else to baby-sit the ashes. I'm driving the kid into Granby."

"You leave here tonight, don't bother coming back."

Uncaring of how they might interpret the gesture, Michael wrapped his arm around Nicki's waist, forcing her to take a step past the foreman who was standing belligerently in front of them. He needed to get her into the pickup and then get the hell out of here before somebody decided to do something overtly hostile.

More hostile than arson and attempted murder?

"You leave with McAdams, boy, and you got no more job on the Half Spur."

Nicki stopped, turning to face the foreman while staying within the support of Michael's arm.

"Somebody tampered with the lock on my door. It wasn't the heat. The fire had just touched the back of the trailer when they locked me in. I'd think you'd be more interested in finding out who did that than in issuing threats."

"Don't you talk to me like that. Not and expect to keep your job," Quarrels blustered.

"Give it to the next poor sucker who's so down on his luck that this place is the best he can do."

"I was good to you."

"You aren't good to anybody," Nicki denied. "We're all dispensable to you. It won't take you long to find somebody to replace me."

She began to move forward again, leaning heavily on Michael's arm. If he hadn't been afraid to leave her alone, he would have gone to get the pickup and come back for her. With what had happened tonight, that wasn't an option.

So they walked on, his limping gait matching her now slowed stride. They passed Mapes, hovering near the burned-out shell of the trailer that had undoubtedly held everything he owned.

Michael knew, with a certainty that made his throat

close, that as soon as those ruins cooled enough to allow it, Ralph would be searching through the rubble for anything he could salvage. The old man, intent on the destruction of what was left of his world, didn't even look up as they trudged by.

IT TOOK MICHAEL less than ten minutes to throw everything he'd brought to the Half Spur back into his bag. In the course of packing, he discovered that someone had searched his belongings again. It didn't matter, since he'd already hidden the blood samples in a security box hidden in the truck.

Nicki sat on the edge of the bunk watching as he cleaned out the small chest, tossing socks and jeans and underwear into the waiting bag. Periodically she coughed or cleared her raw, smoke-damaged throat.

"What now?" she'd asked finally as he'd opened and shut drawers and cabinets one last time in an effort to make sure they were as empty as the day he'd moved in.

Less than two weeks ago, he realized with a sense of wonder. It felt like a lifetime.

"We deliver the samples in person," he said, unwilling to think much past getting her away from here.

He had known from the time she'd whispered her accusation that he was going to take her to the Royal Flush, but he had yet to acknowledge the significance of that. All he had admitted to himself was that he was again going home after another failed mission. Cutting his losses and admitting defeat. And it wasn't any easier because he'd now had some practice at it.

"And then?"

"We see how things have developed on the other fronts, I guess."

"What other fronts?"

"I was sent here to see if there was any connection between this place and the missing Langworthy baby."

"Langworthy as in *the* Langworthys?"

"Gettys's rival," he explained, throwing the strap of the duffel bag over his shoulder.

"What baby?"

"It's a long story," he said, holding out his hand. "I'll tell you on the way."

She put her fingers in his, but she made no move to rise, simply holding them instead. At least hers had stopped shaking.

"You came in to find me, didn't you? I haven't thanked you for that."

"I was the first one there," he said.

"Implying that *anyone* would have come into a burning trailer? One that was equipped with a propane tank?"

"We have to go," he said, ignoring her question as he applied an upward pressure to the hand he held.

She responded by getting up off the bunk, but she didn't move forward.

"Thank you," she repeated.

"Come on."

She didn't refuse this time, but released his hand to lead the way to the door and down the steps. He threw the bag into the back of the pickup before he opened the passenger door and helped her inside. The pall of smoke left from the fire hung heavy on the night air.

Before he closed the door, he leaned inside to secure the seat belt around her body. As he did, she put her head back against the seat and closed her eyes.

He had already stepped away from the car when something about her face, cruelly exposed by the truck's unshielded dome light, stopped him. He ducked his head, inserting the upper half of his body inside the cab again.

Her eyes opened when she felt his movement. He put his hand against her cheek, his thumb on the other side of her chin, and gently turned her face toward him. He studied her features in the too-revealing glare before he bent forward the few inches required to fit his mouth over hers.

For a heartbeat she failed to respond. Then her lips opened under his, warm and sensuous. Tasting of smoke.

The brief kiss was devoid of passion. It was more a benediction. Almost reverent. When it was over, her fingers lay along his cheek, which was prickly with late night whiskers.

"No one else would have come inside to find me," she said softly. "No one but you."

"You were safe here until I showed up." He'd been thinking that from the time he'd seen her body crumpled on the floor. There was a sense of relief in putting that guilt into words.

"As long as I was willing to be Nate Beaumont. Until you got here, I didn't realize how unwilling I was to go on playing that role."

"Then I guess it's good we're leaving," he said, smiling at her.

She said nothing, her eyes questioning. Whatever she wanted to ask, she decided not to. Her hand fell, releasing him.

He slammed the door and walked around behind the truck, scanning the area around his trailer. He didn't relax that vigilance until he was in the driver's seat with his own seat belt fastened.

He couldn't believe Quarrels and the others were going to let them go, but as he turned the key in the ignition, it seemed increasingly likely that would be the case. Maybe Quarrels wasn't authorized to act on his own. Maybe he was down at the compound right now, putting in the call to whoever would tell him what to do next. By the time he had that answer, however, they'd be long gone.

He backed the truck into the turnaround, but instead of heading toward the compound and the road that led off the Half Spur, he headed back up the trail they'd just walked down. The pickup's headlights cut like twin lasers through the smoke that drifted in front of them.

"What are you doing?" Nicki asked as they bumped over the uneven ground.

"Going to get Mapes. He can't stay here."

He was aware that she had turned to look at him then, but he kept his eyes focused on the smoke-shrouded darkness in front of them. After a moment, she unbuckled her seat belt and slid across the bench-type seat until she was sitting beside him, her denim clad thigh resting against his.

"Where will you take us?" she asked, as the headlights picked the old man out of the shadows cast by the few remaining trees. He was standing exactly where he'd been when they'd walked past, his eyes on the smoldering ruins of his trailer. Waiting.

"Home," Michael said simply as he pulled the truck up beside Ralph Mapes.

And for the first time in more than a decade, the word felt right on his tongue, and more important, in his heart.

Chapter Fifteen

"We stopped in Granby to get Nicki checked out and to talk to the sheriff about the possibility of arson. Then I brought them here."

Michael raised the bourbon his sister had handed him to his mouth, examining Colleen's face over the rim of the glass as he drank. He couldn't tell from her expression what she thought about his bare-bones recital of events at the Half Spur. Maybe what a mistake she'd made in entrusting any part of the operation to him. He couldn't blame her for that.

"I'm glad you did. I hope you believe me about that, but whether you do or not, remember that this is your home, too. You have a right to bring anyone you wish here."

He hadn't felt that right, not in the long years since his father's will had made his exile from the Royal Flush so public. Maybe Colleen meant what she'd just said. In this case, it hardly mattered because he hadn't had any choice. He'd literally had nowhere else to take them.

"I appreciate that," he said, his tone more grudging than he'd intended. "As soon as this is cleared up, I'm sure Nicki will opt for a return…to her former life."

That hadn't come out exactly as he'd intended. If Colleen noticed the awkward phrasing, she didn't comment.

He continued quickly to cover the gaffe. "Mapes, however... If you could find him some kind of job here, nothing too strenuous, I'd be grateful."

"Consider it done," his sister said. "There's plenty of room in the bunkhouse, and there's always a need for another set of hands. Especially experienced ones."

"I don't know how much work he's capable of right now—"

"Michael," Colleen interrupted before he could add another caveat to his request. "It doesn't matter. He's welcome. Nicki's welcome. And you're *especially* welcome. I have to confess, I've been worried about you. You came here to recover, and I shamelessly took advantage of you."

"As I remember it, I volunteered," he said, ignoring her expression of concern. It was the last thing he needed to hear right now. "And I brought the samples I promised you. They're in the pickup. Quicker than sending them by mail, I guess." He lifted the glass again.

"What happened to your hand?"

He shifted his drink to the left hand, holding out the right, fingers extended. There were a few nicks and scrapes from the work he'd done at the Half Spur. None of them were as noticeable as the angry red marks on the back.

"Nothing serious," he said dismissively.

"Are those burns?"

"Probably."

"Then they *probably* need some antibiotic ointment. Come to the bathroom with me—"

"I'll take care of it later," he said, cutting her short. He didn't want her playing big sister right now. "Why don't I go ahead and take the samples to the CDC."

"We'll take care of those. Shawn's been chomping at the bit for something interesting to do. I think he's feeling left out."

"Anything turn up on the other fronts? News about the baby?"

She shook her head, one quick negative motion, as her lips tightened. "I was hoping for a quick resolution to this, for everyone's sake, but it doesn't look as if that will be the case."

"What can I help with?"

"I can't think of a thing. At least not until we get the results back from the lab at Fort Collins."

Clearly she didn't intend for him to have any further involvement in her investigation. Just as he'd made up his mind to that, she surprised him.

"Would you care to speculate about what's really going on at Gettys's ranch?"

He shook his head, thinking about everything that he'd seen. "I don't have a clue. I *can* tell you that some part of the operation changed after I got there. Given the daylight visit of the helicopter and the subsequent fire, I'd say something made them nervous. Or maybe that was coincidental to my arrival."

"But you don't believe that."

He shook his head again. "I *don't* think it had anything to do with me taking the samples. I don't believe the foreman has a clue about that."

"Then what?"

"Maybe Nicki searching the office. One of his right-hand men caught her in there. Or maybe Mapes talked too much. It's a failing. Maybe he told them I'd been asking questions. I'd like a chance to find out what tipped them off."

"What kind of chance?"

"To go back without Nicki or the old man."

That way he wouldn't have anyone else to worry about. If he couldn't talk his way back into a job on the ranch, he could at least do some exploring on his own, especially now that he was more familiar with the lay of the land. Actually that might be a better plan than hiring on again.

"But you saw no sign that the baby had ever been there?" Colleen asked.

He shook his head again. "I can't see any connection between the two, other than the wool found in the crib. And Gettys's operation certainly isn't the only sheep ranch in Colorado."

"Then why go back?"

"Because it's possible somebody there tried to murder an old man and a woman. And because they're too secretive for something *not* to be going on."

"Something you think has nothing to do with the kidnapping," his sister clarified again.

"That doesn't mean it doesn't need investigating," he insisted stubbornly.

"One windmill at a time," Colleen said, smiling at him. "Colorado Confidential is stretched pretty thin."

"I didn't mean as part of some official investigation. I'd be working on my own."

Another silence, this one tense.

"I don't have any authority over you, and I know that," Colleen said, "but I thought you signed on for this assignment."

"Meaning you're against my going back."

"For now." Her voice was carefully neutral. "First of all, I'd like you to take a couple of days to recuperate."

"I'm fine."

"And then I'd like you to provide security for Nicki," Colleen continued as if he hadn't spoken. "I think she's key to our figuring out what Gettys's involvement in this is. If anything happens to her, our chances for discovering that are considerably lessened."

"Nobody knows she's here. Even if her disguise was penetrated, there's no way to tie her to the Royal Flush."

"Not unless they've tied *you* to the Half Spur."

And had then traced her here because of him? That would mean his visit to the ranch had been an even bigger fiasco than he'd imagined.

"No way," he said, mentally reviewing the precautions he'd taken.

"Nicki had hidden there for months," Colleen reminded him. "Almost as soon as you show up, things start to happen. As you said, a little too coincidental. If, by sending you to the Half Spur, I put her into danger, then I feel responsible for keeping her safe until we figure out how all these seemingly unrelated pieces fit together."

He said nothing, looking down on the remaining bourbon in the bottom of his glass as he tried to work out how Quarrels, or whoever he was working for, could have figured out that the notorious Nicola Carson was hiding in their midst.

"Or do you want me to give the assignment to someone else?"

That threat brought his eyes up. Colleen would do it, he knew. If there was one thing that had been consistent about his sister her entire life, it was her strong sense of responsibility. If she thought their investigation of the Langworthy kidnapping might have inadvertently put Nicki at risk, she'd see to it that Colorado Confidential did everything in their power to make the situation right.

Shawn's been chomping at the bit for something interesting to do, Colleen had said.

Suddenly Michael was determined that Jameson wasn't going to be playing bodyguard to Nicki. If Colleen was serious about the assignment, no one was going to do that but him.

THE DRAPES had been pulled across the wide bedroom windows, but the afternoon sun was too strong and their fabric too sheer to cast the room into darkness. The resulting dimness was soothing, as was the subtle scent of lavender that emanated from the bed linens.

Underlying that was something that suggested citrus. Maybe bath salts, Michael thought, noticing the open bathroom door.

That would have been the first thing Nicki did after their arrival. Wash off the stench of smoke. And along with it, he hoped, the horror of being locked inside that inferno.

The quiet luxury of the guest suite seemed a world away from the deprivations of the Half Spur. He'd only spent a couple of weeks there. He couldn't imagine how she must feel to have finally escaped.

He crossed to the bed, bootheels silent over the lush carpeting. He stood looking down on her as she slept, feeling a little like a voyeur, but unwilling to deny himself the pleasure.

Her face, totally relaxed in sleep, seemed almost childlike. Devoid of makeup, hair badly cropped, there was still an innate femininity in her features that made him wonder how in the world she had fooled Quarrels and his cronies so long.

She had washed most of the artificial color from her hair. Not as pale as the line of silver-gilt he'd glimpsed that first day, it was definitely blond again and tousled artlessly around her face. Unable to resist, he reached down and swept a strand away from her temple.

His fingers looked dark and rough against the smoothness of her skin. His hand was still hovering in midair when she moved.

Rolling onto her back, she looked up at him, eyes wide,

though clouded with sleep. As soon as she recognized him, her lips tilted, aligning into a smile.

He let his hand fall to his side. He met her eyes, hiding nothing, but he refused to allow his mouth to respond to the curve of hers. After a second or two, her smile faded.

"What's wrong?" she asked.

"Colleen thinks you should stay here for a while."

There was a small silence as she thought about it.

"And you object to that?"

"I thought you might."

"Someone tried to kill me. I still don't know who or why. Until I do… I have nowhere else to go."

He nodded as if she'd just agreed to something.

"She asked me to look after you."

For some reason, the blue eyes filled with moisture, just as they had on the trail that day. Blinking to control the tears, Nicki reached up and took the hand with which he'd brushed the tendril away from her face.

Her gaze touched on the burn marks before it lifted to his face. "You've already been doing that."

"Not in any official capacity."

"And this is official?"

He gently freed his fingers before he answered. "Colleen runs an investigative agency that operates under the auspices of the Department of Public Safety. Until they complete their investigation of the Langworthy kidnapping, she wants you under protection."

"You work for her."

"For now."

"And all those other things you told me—"

"Part of my checkered past. I thought I'd retired."

"Because of your knee."

"Among other things."

When she spoke again, it wasn't, thankfully, to ask what those "things" were.

"Then why do this? Why go to the Half Spur?"

Because some hotshot implied I wasn't up to it.

"Colleen needed an operative," he said.

"That's what you were? An operative?"

"Whatever I was, I'm not any longer."

"Just...my bodyguard."

"For the time being."

"To protect me from Gettys?"

"To protect you from anyone who might want to harm you."

"Believe me, there isn't anyone else who would want to do that. I'm not the kind of person who has enemies. Frankly, I'm not all that interesting."

It was as if she'd forgotten what he'd told her about the call-girl ring. He wanted to believe that was because it wasn't true, but a splinter of doubt still festered in the back of his mind.

At least now that he was back at the Royal Flush, he could use his own contacts to check out that story. They were far better than those Colleen had been relying on.

"You were interesting to someone," he said.

"Gettys," she insisted. "It has to be. And despite those endless months on the Half Spur, I'm no closer to knowing why than I was then."

"If Gettys is involved in any of this, it will come out. Colleen is sending the blood samples we took to the CDC. We should have their report in a few days. The lab we found will be on the CIA's satellite photographs. If no one's investigated it before, they will now. There's too much concern about bioterrorism these days for them not to."

"Is *that* what you think is going on at the Half Spur? Some kind of…biological weapons research?"

"Not judging by the caliber of the hired help."

That reality provoked another smile. This one displayed amusement rather than the unspoken invitation he'd seen in the first. "Don't tell me you doubt Charlie's intelligence."

"Among other things."

"He was smart enough to keep me from figuring out what was going on," she said with a touch of bitterness.

"I know it's hard not to know why you became a target. And probably harder to have to trust someone else to get to the bottom of it, but I hope you will."

"Do *you* trust them?"

It was a fair question and not easy to answer. Colleen was the only one of the team he really knew. He had no doubt his sister had been a good cop. No doubt about her dedication or her intelligence or her competence. What he couldn't know was whether or not her agents shared those attributes.

"All I can tell you is that if they don't get to the bottom of it, I will," he vowed.

Nothing like making a promise you aren't sure you're capable of keeping.

Despite his having left the Half Spur with a lot of things unresolved, the experience had at least assured him that physically he was recovered enough to do whatever he had to. He might be slower, and the aftermath might be unpleasant, but there hadn't been a single time when his knee had kept him from doing what needed to be done.

"That's good enough for me," Nicki said softly. "Thank you."

Another silence, this one stretching long enough to become awkward. Of course, he was in her bedroom. Uninvited. Probably unwanted.

"I'll let you rest," he said. "I didn't mean to wake you."

"Just checking to make sure I was still breathing?" she asked, her lips curving again. Almost teasing. "All part of the job."

The reason he was here had nothing to do with "the job," and everything to do with his confusion over his feelings for her. And until those had been resolved—

He should warn her of what he intended to do, he realized. The people he wanted to call to investigate those stories about Nicola Carson would leave no stone in her past unturned. She should be made aware of their thoroughness.

In case there's some little something she hasn't told you?

"I'm going to ask a couple of former associates for help in identifying the people who targeted you in Washington. You should know that they'll also delve extensively into your private life. You may not be comfortable with that, but it will be almost impossible to figure out who sent your assailant that night without considering everyone you know as suspects. Unless, of course, the attack was random."

"It wasn't. I told you that. And it wasn't a robbery."

"Then somebody had to have a very good reason to want you dead."

The blue eyes lost focus for a moment. She seemed to be thinking about what he'd said. Or maybe she was trying to come up with someone who fit that description.

"Tell them to delve away," she said after a moment, meeting his eyes. "While they're at it, tell them I'd like to know who started the rumor you heard."

His stomach tightened reactively. This wasn't territory he was ready to deal with again. "About the videotapes?"

"All of it. Everything you were told. Every sordid detail. That *has* to be connected to the attack because none of it's true. If they're going to be examining my acquaintances, that should be uncovered pretty quickly."

He nodded. "I'll tell them. Sorry I woke you."

He had already turned to leave when her question stopped him. "Have you slept?"

He had driven the entire way back to the ranch. For most of the journey Ralph had leaned against the passenger-side door, softly snoring as the miles rolled by. Nicki had stayed awake, but they hadn't talked, each lost in their private reflections about the events of the night.

"I'll sleep later."

"Are you working?"

"Right now?" He shook his head.

"Then…" She took a breath, her eyes holding his. Before she formed the words, he knew what she was about to say. And his gut knotted in anticipation of hearing it. "Could you stay here?"

The silence was again strained.

"I don't think that would be a good idea," he said truthfully.

She didn't deny what he'd suggested. She reached for his hand instead, and seemingly paralyzed, he let her lift it as she had before. She held his fingers a moment before she ran her thumb across the back of it, right above the knuckles, lightly touching the burns.

"I can't help thinking about what would have happened if you hadn't come for me," she said.

"Someone would have."

She shook her head. "You know that isn't true. Even if it were, it doesn't make the nightmares go away."

"Neither can I." *Not even my own.*

"That's a chance I'm willing to take," she said.

It would be sheer stupidity, even given the charge Colleen had handed him only minutes ago. That argument, however reasoned, didn't have any effect on his body's reaction.

He wanted her. He had since the night he'd first kissed her, furious over the allegations she'd just given him permission to have investigated.

He pulled his hand from hers. Watching the change in her face as he did, that was as far as his resistance went.

That's a chance I'm willing to take.

He was the risk taker. The adrenaline junky. This was just another kind of risk. Far less dangerous than those he'd taken in the past. Far more tempting.

Maybe she meant what she said. Maybe all she wanted from him was someone to keep the bad dreams at bay. He couldn't fault her for that. If that was as far as this went…

He had nightmares of his own. And enough lonely nights to last a lifetime. He wasn't looking forward to another.

Chapter Sixteen

Eyes open, she lay in the twilight, listening to the comforting sound of Michael's breathing. Relishing the slow, steady rhythm of it. It was all that had allowed her to sleep through the long afternoon.

She knew what he'd thought when she asked him to stay. And she wouldn't have objected had this turned into something other than what she'd suggested. After all, *she* hadn't been the one who had pulled away before.

Although she no longer bothered to deny the depth of her attraction to this man, she couldn't begin to explain it. She had never before allowed anyone to treat her with the kind of disrespect he'd shown her. The only rationale she could come up with for her willingness to forgive his behavior was that she knew he'd been operating under a lot of misconceptions.

And maybe the fact that he'd saved her life at the risk of his own had something to do with it, too, she acknowledged ruefully.

It hadn't taken her long to figure out that his sister must be the one who'd told him that garbage about the videotapes. "The people he worked for" had been a convenient euphemism for Colleen Wellesley's agency.

Michael would never dream of questioning his sister's

word. Or taking a stranger's over it. That Nicki was telling the truth about her life in Washington was something he was going to have to verify for himself.

She had already discovered he wasn't someone who trusted easily. Neither was she. Not anymore. Present company excepted, of course.

Besides, if Michael's sources were as good as he claimed, it wouldn't take them long to clear her name. She wasn't a complete innocent, but her life had been so far removed from the kind of things that had been suggested to him that it shouldn't take much of an investigation to prove it.

All she had to do was be patient. Something at which she'd had a great deal of practice during the past few months. More than she had wanted.

There was a subtle change in the pattern of Michael's breathing. Although she had discovered during the long afternoon what a dangerous temptation looking at him could be, it was one she didn't try to resist.

She turned her head to find that he was lying on his side facing her. In the faint light she could see smudges of exhaustion beneath the long dark lashes.

She wondered if the lines that furrowed his brow, even while he slept, were signs of pain or anxiety. Maybe both. Along with the day-old growth of beard that covered his lean cheeks, they should have detracted from his looks. They didn't. Not in any way. Not to her. After all, those signs of exhaustion had been acquired on her behalf.

Suddenly his eyes opened, almost as if in response to her unguarded scrutiny. He said nothing, simply looking back at her. In the room's near darkness, his irises were luminous, their color the clear blue-green of an ocean far beyond the breakers.

She wanted to reach out and touch him. To put her hand

on his cheek. Or to take his fingers into hers again. To reestablish some physical contact between them.

That's why she had responded so quickly to him that night in his trailer. For days as they'd worked side by side, she had wanted to touch him. To have him touch her. And when it had finally happened, it had felt so right.

Until he pushed you away.

He had. And for that reason she couldn't make the first advance tonight. Not beyond what she'd already done in asking him to stay. The next move would have to be up to him.

Fool me once…

Now she was waiting, in near breathless anticipation, for him to do that again.

He pushed up onto one elbow, raising his torso so that he was looking down at her. His eyes considered her face a long time, studying her features as if he had never before seen them. Then he leaned forward, his mouth slowly lowering toward hers.

She raised her hand, putting her fingers over his lips. "Don't," she said softly.

His forward motion stopped. His head tilted slightly. Questioning the command.

"Not if this is going to be like before," she said. "If what your sister told you is going to make you treat me as if I'm guilty as charged, then we stop now."

"Stop what?"

He lifted his chin enough to take her fingers into his mouth. He held them a moment and then released them, leaning back again to drop kisses along the tips. There was a shift in the bottom of her stomach as something molten, hot and liquid, stirred to life.

"Whatever that was about to be." Her voice sounded thready to her own ears.

"A kiss?" he asked innocently.

She nodded, still holding his eyes.

"You object to me kissing you?"

"I object to you always starting something and then running away."

"You think that's what I've been doing? Running away?"

"Isn't it?"

At least he was thinking about it. She could see the thoughts moving behind those remarkable eyes.

"I didn't want to think about what they'd said. I couldn't stand the thought that it might be true," he said. "And no, I can't explain to you why that was so important to me. It shouldn't have been."

"It would have been important to me."

"If I'd had a checkered past?"

The same words that he'd used to describe his own.

"*That* kind of past."

"There are worse kinds."

She swallowed, thinking of the little he'd told her about his. Military intelligence. CIA. For the first time she began to wonder about what he might *not* have told her.

There *were* far worse things than what she'd been accused of. Things she wouldn't want to know about if he'd done them. In her case, however—

"I'm going to say this for the last time," she said, putting all the conviction she could into her voice. "What Colleen told you isn't true. None of it. I swear that to you. I can't do anything about whether or not you believe me, but I *am* telling you the truth."

He nodded, his eyes serious. The lines that bracketed his lips seemed more deeply graven than they had been before; the circles under his eyes pronounced, despite his nap.

"Then I'll say *this* for the first and the last time, too.

Whatever you just imagined pales in comparison to the reality.''

The reality of who and what Michael Wellesley was.

He'd been a CIA operative. She had never thought about what that meant until he forced her to.

Spying? Nothing she would consider dishonorable, not if one did it for one's country.

She tried to think what she knew about other CIA activities. Antiterrorism, which was a good thing, of course. Arranging coups to topple foreign governments? At least they had in the past. Assassinations? By law, they couldn't do that anymore. Or did they still do it and just not tell anyone?

''*All* of it's true,'' he said as if he could read her thoughts.

''Is that supposed to scare me?'' she asked with a hint of defiance.

''Does it?''

On some level it did, and she wasn't sure why. She had trusted him with her life. She would again. How could it frighten her that he was both capable of and willing to do anything to protect her?

''No,'' she lied.

''Then explain why the hell it bothers me so much to think about you selling your body?''

Because you can't bear that sordidness to be the reality for someone you love.

That was the only reason that made sense. The idea that she'd sold her body wouldn't bother him unless he cared about her. Definitely not something she could say aloud. Not now. There were, however, other things she could say.

''I don't know why it should or shouldn't bother you, and I don't really care. Because that *isn't* my reality. It never has been. So you can put it out of your mind. Along with whatever other gossip Colleen told you about me. Anyway, aren't you a little *old* to be working for your sister?'' she finished, her voice rising.

Whatever reaction she'd expected, it wasn't what she got. She didn't think she'd ever seen him laugh. And that was a pity, she decided.

When the sound of it had faded, another of those small, awkward silences was left behind. The kind that occurred when two people don't know one another as well as they pretend they do. His eyes were serious again, intently focused on her face.

''So what happens if I promise no more running away?''

For a moment she was at a loss, until she remembered that's what she'd accused him of. Making a move, convincing her that this time it would all be different, and then stopping. Running away. If not physically, at least psychologically.

Fool me twice...

''Are you? Promising that, I mean?''

''Isn't that what you wanted?''

You're what I wanted.

But not if it's going to be like before. He had hurt and humiliated her, and she wasn't going to let it happen again.

''If you can't accept what I've told you as the truth,'' she said, ''then it would be better for both of us to have this conversation *after* your sources have verified my veracity.''

She watched his eyes. No trace of laughter lingered there. His mouth was set, almost stern.

As the silence built, she wondered what she'd do if he got up to leave. Would she have enough pride to let him walk out? And if he did, would she ever again be willing to have this conversation, no matter what she'd just said? Would he?

She knew she was asking him to take a lot on faith. To believe her rather than Colleen and the media. To believe her about something for which she could offer no proof.

"That wasn't an ultimatum," she began. "I know it must have sounded like one—"

She stopped because he was leaning forward again. She waited, lips parted on the unfinished sentence, as his mouth descended to hers.

He had kissed her before, but this was nothing like those. This was the sweet, almost tentative joining of lips she had expected the first time.

And after he had touched his mouth to hers, the pressure light and undemanding, he leaned back an inch or two. Far enough that she could look into his eyes.

"I'm not going anywhere," he said.

She took a breath, more ragged and revealing than she had intended, and then succumbed to the temptation she had resisted before. She put her palm against his check, enjoying the quintessentially male roughness of his beard beneath it.

She lowered her eyes, deliberately breaking that powerful contact between them, to watch her thumb trace over the fullness of his bottom lip. When she raised them again, his face was exactly the same.

Composed. Serious. And waiting.

"Me either," she said. "Not until you tell me I have to."

AT SOME POINT during the night, she had found herself wondering what Colleen thought about their long absence. The curiosity had been fleeting, as were most of the questions she'd entertained during the brief intervals when she was capable of coherent thought, but it filled her with an ironic amusement.

Michael's sister believed she was sexually experienced. After tonight, that was not a claim she would dare dispute, although her experience had not been acquired in the way that Colleen imagined.

Whatever you just imagined…

Michael's words echoed in her head, and she realized that what she'd fantasized about their lovemaking had not matched the reality, either. *The reality of Michael Wellesley.*

A man so secure in his own control, she had felt no need to do anything other than surrender to it. A man so comfortable with his own sensuality that she was free to indulge hers. A man who made love with the same physical prowess he had demonstrated since the day he'd disarmed her and thrown her to the ground in one smoothly choreographed motion.

Throughout the night he had given her incredible pleasure. Seemingly because he enjoyed doing that, certainly without demanding anything in return. Nothing but her willing submission to his guidance.

He had been totally attuned to every nuance of her response. Each shuddering breath had called forth a renewed effort to evoke the next. Each whispered confession of need was followed by another demand on her body, which in turn created another, yet more powerful need. He had answered each one, exceeding every expectation she had ever had.

Now she lay, completely relaxed, her body spooned into his, again listening to him breathe. This time, however, she could also feel each rise and fall of his chest.

Despite the passion they had shared throughout the long hours, despite their continued proximity, that nearness evoked nothing but an exhausted contentment. She was completely sated. Every centimeter of her skin had been sensitized by the slow caress of his lips and tongue and by the knowing touch of long, dark fingers. Every bone, muscle and sinew had been marked with his possession. Every atom of her being satiated with his lovemaking.

He had not been gentle, but she hadn't expected him to be. He wasn't a gentle man. She had known that and had been prepared for his dominance.

What she hadn't been prepared for—couldn't have been because it was so outside the realm of her experience—was what he was capable of making her feel. And say. And do.

Things she had never done in her entire life. Had never before even *thought* about doing.

Here with him those acts had become as natural as drawing breath. As right. As necessary. And she had not once considered refusing.

She turned within the circle of his arms. He shifted a little in his sleep to allow her change of positions, as if they had slept together every night of their lives, and then pulled her into a frontal embrace.

She settled against him, her breasts pressed against his chest. Despite her exhaustion, the sensuous abrasion of the coarse hair that covered it sent flickers of sensation, as quick and heated as summer lightning, running throughout her body.

She denied them, pushing them from her mind as she burrowed tiredly into his warmth. Her head rested on his shoulder, their bodies touching along their entire lengths. She put her knee atop his thigh, aware again of the sheer masculinity of hair-roughened skin sheathing strength beneath.

She sighed soundlessly, consciously relaxing into the new position with the intention of going back to sleep. A small adjustment of the leg that lay over his. A repositioning of her arm. A yawn.

At the end of it, his mouth found hers. Opened. Vulnerable. Taken by surprise.

As he kissed her, his hand covered the small of her back, his callused palm settling between the twin indentions on either side of her spine. He applied pressure with the obvious intent of urging her closer. Given the position of her thigh on top of his, the outcome of the maneuver, intentional or not, could be nothing less than an increased intimacy.

And despite the number of times they had made love, she could feel the quick, responsive stirring of his erection. Surprisingly, there was a matching flutter of excitement deep within her own body. Apparently she was not so sated as she had believed.

He deepened the kiss. At the same time he slipped his hand around her knee, the one that lay over his. He hooked his forearm under it, carrying her leg upward.

His erection lay against the exposed heart of her sexuality. Given the backdrop of what they had shared tonight, there was no further need of stimulation.

A rush of hot moisture released in anticipation of his invasion, but again he surprised her. He rolled onto his back, carrying her with him.

The knee he'd moved now rested on the mattress beside his hip. The other fell into place on the opposite side. The hand that had been against her spine supported her until she was sitting upright, astride his body.

She realized that this was one of the few ways they had not made love. And she understood why. He was a man who needed to be in control. A man who took control.

Now he had relinquished it to her. An action as deliberate as any he'd made last night.

As she looked down into his eyes, his mouth curved into a slow smile. Invitation? Or challenge?

She leaned forward, resting her palms on his chest so that they were eye-to-eye. Almost nose-to-nose.

"Ever break a horse to saddle?" he asked.

"No," she said, "but I've ridden a mule or two in my day."

He laughed. "In Washington?"

"On my daddy's farm."

He nodded as if what she'd said meant something. He had never asked about her background, but perhaps he'd wondered.

"What's it like riding a mule?"

"They're ornery and stubborn and occasionally they need reasoning with to make them see the error of their ways."

"You any good at that?"

"Reasoning or riding?"

"What do you think?"

HE WATCHED HER in the early morning light, her hands on his waist, her head thrown back so that the smooth column of her neck was exposed. The powerful muscles in her thighs, strengthened from months of work on the ranch, controlled the movements that were driving him nearer and nearer to the edge of the abyss.

He tried to think about something else. Anything else. Anything but this.

He reached up to touch the locket that lay between her breasts, fingers trembling against the damp satin of her skin. She had told him it was a family heirloom, the only tangible connection she had left to her heritage.

Nicki's head came up, her eyes opened to look down into his. They were glazed. Unseeing. She closed her mouth, running the tip of her tongue around her lips. The rise and fall of her hips never faltered.

There were things that he needed to say. Things he should tell her, but the words were lodged in the back of his brain, all his powers of concentration focused on another kind of communication. One at which they had grown very skilled.

He couldn't remember ever letting a woman make love to him. And there was no doubt that's what she had done. She had touched him in ways that were intimate beyond belief. Yet there had been nothing practiced in what she had done. Nothing that had reawakened the doubts.

It had been clear she made love to him because she wanted to. A gift she gave him because she wanted him to feel exactly as he now did. As though they were intimately connected, and not only in the physical sense, although he couldn't deny the obvious reality of that.

This was something deeper. Something…spiritual. And he'd never felt that with another woman.

He released the locket to draw the tips of his fingers down her body, tracing a line from the pulsing hollow of her throat, between the globes of her breasts, and then lower still. Trailing across the small, slightly convex curve of her belly.

His hand hesitated there, his mind picturing smooth, white skin stretched tautly over the growing body of his son or daughter. Because of the inherent danger in what he did, he had never thought about having children. Except now…

He could see her carrying his child. Her body swollen with his seed. Her face glowing with the promise of that.

A promise he had never before wanted. One that he knew was the proper culmination of what they had found together.

The connection had been there from the first. They had fought against it because there had been other battles demanding their concentration. Other adversaries. There still were.

She raised and then lowered her body again. The same tantalizing motion that sheathed the length of his erection in wet heat. So wet that at the peak of each lift, he felt a momentary anxiety that she would lift too far. That she would leave him, if only briefly.

It hadn't happened, and he knew that in a few seconds it wouldn't matter. Whatever control he had once had over his own body was spiraling away.

Evaporating like a single raindrop against the heat of a desert rock. Then the droplets would fall closer and closer together, each adding to the accumulation until there was no distinction between them.

Just as there was no break in the rhythm she had established. No chance between those downward strokes to gather his resolve to hold on until she could join him.

He closed his eyes, struggling to contain the welling flood of sensation that clamored for release. His hand slid down the last few inches to touch the spot where their bodies joined.

As it did, he felt the tremors begin in the slim, beautiful body straining above him. He put his hands on her waist again. He heard the breath she took, one long gasping inhalation before the internal cataclysm began.

Her body rocked over his, oblivious now to his reaction. Free at last of the need to control his own responses, he exploded inside her, his hips answering the demand of hers.

He had no idea how long it lasted. An instant. An eternity.

And as it faded, he could again hear the harshness of his own breathing. In the background of that he was aware she was saying something as she continued to climax. And not a single word of it could his brain grasp.

Or maybe there weren't any words. Perhaps she was as inarticulate as he, just as the hot stream of his ejaculation seemed unending.

Gradually the frantic pace eased. Heat quenched. Muscles relaxed from near convulsion.

She leaned forward against his chest. He kissed her hair, which smelled of summer, and then pressed his lips over the sweat-dampened skin at her temple. It was salt-sweet, warm against his tongue.

Her hand lifted to cup his cheek. He turned his head and kissed her palm.

"Thank you," he said.

She raised her body away from his, looking down into his face. "For what? Or should I be thanking you, too?"

"For holding nothing back."

The words didn't begin to convey what he was feeling. He couldn't find any others, however, so he let them stand.

"That was never an option."

"In my experience, it's always an option."

"I defer to your superior knowledge, of course, but… Maybe it's different when you care about someone."

He nodded. When she didn't go on, he realized she was waiting for some response from him. Although he had already acknowledged that what they had together was vastly different from anything he'd ever known before and that he needed to tell her that, still he said nothing.

"Obviously riding," she said softly.

"What?"

"The one I'm better at." She laid her head on his chest again.

Next time, he vowed, as his lips brushed over her hair. Next time he'd say the words she wanted to hear. Next time.

Chapter Seventeen

"Those test results *still* aren't back from the CDC."

After a quick glance at his sister's face, Michael went back to saddling the bay and white paint he'd been given permission to exercise in Night Walker's absence.

"Maybe that means they've found something interesting," he said easily, his hands moving through the routine tasks with a competence that years away from the ranch didn't seem to have compromised.

"Maybe we should have given them more information," Colleen said, her brow furrowing as it did when she was worrying.

"What exactly did Shawn tell them?"

"That the blood had been taken from a flock which was supposedly part of a government research program."

"Maybe that's the holdup. If they're trying to match whatever they found in those samples to a protocol database—"

He stopped when he spotted Nicki coming toward them from the house. She'd trimmed her hair so that it shaped her face in a much more feminine style, and the tight-fitting jeans and shirt she wore emphasized her curves. Again he wondered how she'd ever managed to convince anyone she was a boy.

He wondered where the clothing had come from, as they hadn't set foot off the property since their arrival. Of course, Nicki had immediately been taken under the wing of Colleen's motherly housekeeper, Melody Castillo. It was possible the garments belonged to Melody's grandsons, who were both tall and slim enough to be a physical match for Nicki.

"Ready?" he called, noting the hesitation in her stride as she realized Colleen was here.

Maybe she was afraid their morning ride together was about to be aborted. It had quickly become a ritual. One they both looked forward to as a chance to get away from the curiosity of the members of the household.

Colleen's eyes touched briefly on his, that anxious wrinkle still disturbing her brow, before she turned to smile a welcome. Although Nicki had been at the ranch for almost a week, the relationship between the two women had not progressed beyond the pleasant civility of their first meeting.

For Colleen's part, he believed that was because he hadn't yet received any further information about the call-girl accusations. With remarkable restraint, neither she nor Nicki had yet asked what his sources had told him, but he was expecting their questions any day.

He certainly understood how much Nicki wanted to clear her reputation. Once that was out of the way, he hoped the strain between her and his sister would ease.

"Good morning," Colleen said as their guest drew near.

"Colleen," Nicki said with a nod.

He thought the response seemed cool, but then he'd noticed the same standoffishness on his sister's part before. As sensitive as Nicki was, she had obviously picked up on that. Maybe he needed to arrange some opportunities for them to get to know each other better, considering his rapidly developing feelings for her.

"Why don't you join us, Colleen?" he asked, watching the sudden dilation of Nicki's eyes. Whatever she was thinking, however, she hid it well, turning to add her invitation to his.

"Dex would have my hide," Colleen said. "He doesn't think I do enough work around here anyway. I promised him I'd ride into Denver with him this morning. There's a bull he wants me to take a look at."

Michael wondered if his sister was really unaware that the foreman's constant demands on her time stemmed less from his desire for her input in the running of the ranch than from his personal desire to spend time with her. It hadn't taken him long to figure out that Dex Jones's interest wasn't entirely professional, but Colleen seemed oblivious to his attraction to her.

"Why don't you take Ralph with you?" he suggested. "He's forgotten more about cattle than you and Dex ever knew."

Besides, the old man hadn't been off the ranch since they'd arrived. He seemed to have recovered from whatever illness had sapped his strength during the last few days on the Half Spur. He was back to normal, talkative and almost jovial, enjoying the thought of Nicki fooling Quarrels for so long. Trading that hellhole for the Royal Flush definitely agreed with him.

As it had with all of them, he thought, considering the woman standing confidently beside Colleen. Of course there might be more involved in Nicki's case than a change of environment. Or that might just be his ego talking again.

"I'll ask him," Colleen agreed. "Have fun, you two. And while you're doing it, think about those of us who have to work for a living."

He wondered if there was supposed to be a hidden meaning in the words. Or even a not-so-subtle double entendre.

After he and Nicki watched his sister cross the yard and head back toward the house, she turned to him, her face tight. "Maybe she wanted you to go in to Denver with them."

"She doesn't need my help. Doesn't want it either. Besides, I have a job. One she assigned."

"Why wouldn't she want it?" Nicki asked, ignoring the other. "I would think running an operation this size would be a big job for anybody. Now that you're home, she'd probably welcome—"

"My father left the ranch to Colleen in his will." Despite his belief that he had overcome the old bitterness, there was still a quiver of resentment as he said the word.

"He cut you out of his will?"

Nicki sounded as if she had a hard time believing his father would do that. Of course, so had he.

"He gave me money, but none of the land."

"But…why?"

"He thought I didn't value it. Not like Colleen did."

"Was he right?"

His lips flattened before he forced them opened to say, the single syllable abrupt, "No."

"Then—"

"He never asked me," Michael said. As if that explained anything. "If he had, I would have told him how I felt."

She didn't state the obvious, even though she was undoubtedly thinking it. *Why didn't you just tell him without being asked?* He'd asked himself that same question a thousand times. And had wondered how different his life would have turned out if he had.

"WHY DO I FEEL as if we're sneaking off like a couple of teenagers?" Nicki asked.

She reached up to push a strand of hair off his forehead, smiling into his eyes as she did. And despite the time they'd spent together during the past few days—or maybe because of it—her throat went dry in expectation.

"Because that's exactly what we're doing?" Michael suggested.

"And all those perfectly good beds back at the ranch going to waste."

While he'd staked the horses, she had spread out the blanket he'd carried behind his saddle on a flat, granite boulder. The rock, pleasantly warm from the sun, was partially shaded now. She had already been lying on top of it when Michael joined her.

"Too many people. Here…" He shrugged, not bothering to state the obvious.

"And I always feel as if Colleen disapproves of our spending time together."

Nicki had been unable to resist making that observation despite her determination not to talk about his sister. Especially not out here. This was the one place where she didn't feel as if Colleen were watching and judging everything they did.

She had tried to be patient, knowing that when Michael's former colleagues finished their inquiries, there would be a positive resolution of the questions Colleen had raised about her past. And for her that couldn't come too soon.

Even if they didn't talk about it, however, his sister's disapproval seemed to hover around them like a fog. If there had been anywhere else half as safe, she would have urged Michael to leave the ranch with her. As it was, she said as little as possible about the media stories Colleen had relayed to him, knowing that eventually she would be vindicated.

"It's not you," he said, dismissing her concern with an easy assurance. "Colleen's worried about the Langworthy mess. This is the first high-profile case her team's been asked to handle, and the investigation appears to be going nowhere. At least it seems that way to her. The longer that baby is missing, the more tense Colleen is going to become. It isn't personal, believe me."

If only I could, Nicki thought.

"Besides, looking after you is my job," he continued, leaning down to drop a kiss on the tip of her nose. "She's not going to question the amount of time we spend together."

Nicki wondered if he really didn't sense what she did in Colleen's attitude or if he were only trying to keep the peace. Then, as his lips fastened over hers, she gladly put the problem from her mind. His sister might be Michael's boss, but despite that, Nicki knew him well enough by now to know that he would do whatever he thought best in this situation.

In *any* situation, she amended. Michael didn't seem overly concerned about maintaining the chain of command. Maybe that was the one advantage to be found in this kind of nepotism.

She put her hand on the back of his neck, threading her fingers through the dark hair that curled over his collar. After all, there was no reason to waste a perfectly good morning worrying about something she couldn't change. Especially not when there were so many more pleasant things to occupy it.

His fingers had found the top button of the shirt she wore, working to slip it out of its hole. While he unfastened the rest, not hurrying over the task, his lips and tongue explored the sensitive skin along her throat.

When all the buttons had been undone, he tried to tug the tail of the shirt out of the waistband of her borrowed jeans. Unfortunately, they fit so well that proved impossible.

''Wait,'' she said.

With the intention of taking off both the shirt and her bra, she put her hand against his chest, pushing him back a little so she could sit up. Just as she moved, something hit her in the back of the shoulder.

The blow was powerful and unexpected. Her first thought was that she'd been struck by a rattler, although she hadn't heard the infamous warning. A fraction of a second later, she recognized a very different sound. The unmistakable report of a high-powered rifle echoed off the rocks.

In the same instant her mind made that identification, Michael rolled off the blanket and the rock, carrying her with him. The drop to the ground was jarring, although he had used his own body to cushion her fall. As soon as they landed, he reversed the direction of the roll, taking them back into the shadow of the boulder, using the rock to shield them from the shooter.

Instinctively, she raised her head, trying to locate whoever had fired at them. Michael's hand between her shoulder blades forced her back to the ground.

''Stay down,'' he hissed. The Glock, carried in a holster in the small of his back, was already in the other hand.

She watched as he visually searched the ridge that lay to their left. Working from the trajectory of the bullet that had struck her, he must believe that was the vantage point from which the gunman had fired.

The glimpse she'd caught before Michael had shoved her down revealed a forbidding landscape of irregular outcroppings and scrub vegetation. And a hundred places where a would-be assassin might hide.

Would-be assassin. When the words formed in her brain, she knew that what she had anticipated with such dread all those months on the Half Spur had finally come to pass. The man who had tried to kill her in Washington had found her.

"It's him," she whispered.

Despite Michael's warning, she raised her head a few inches to look up at him. Breaking his concentration on the ridge, he turned toward her. He didn't bother to deny what she said.

"What do we do?" she asked, trying to examine the injury by feel.

Although she could move the arm, the wound was beginning to hurt—a deep burn, like someone had directed a blowtorch at her flesh. And there was a lot of blood, she realized, looking down on the gory fingers with which she'd just touched the place the bullet had struck her shoulder.

"Let me look at that," Michael said, pushing her back down—gently this time—so he could examine the wound.

She couldn't see his face, but his silence was frightening. After a second or two of prodding, against which she had to lock her teeth in her bottom lip, he began to take off his shirt.

The movement was awkward because of the necessity of staying low, but he managed. He folded the fabric into a small, tight square and laid it against her back, pressing it down firmly. She gasped in response, and the pressure immediately eased.

"Put your hand over it," he ordered, guiding her blood-stained fingers to the pad he'd fashioned. "And press hard. We need to control the bleeding."

She had known that's what he was trying to do, but hearing him put it into words increased the knot of fear growing in her stomach. Because if they couldn't stop it—

She closed her eyes, trying not to think about any of the "what-ifs." She wasn't successful. They were effectively pinned down. Any attempt to move away from the boulder would make them highly visible targets to the man on the ridge.

And no one on the Royal Flush knew where they were. They hadn't mentioned when they could be expected back, so it was unlikely anyone would be worried about their disappearance for hours.

Despite Nicki's impression that Colleen wasn't pleased about the time they were spending together, Michael's sister had made no overt effort to do anything about it. Which meant she wasn't going to come looking for her brother and his guest. Nor would she send anyone else.

Pressing the pad against the wound, she raised her eyes to find that Michael was no longer looking at the ridge. He had turned instead toward the horses, which were staked to their left and the gunman's right, near the bottom of the incline from which he'd fired.

Estimating the distance they'd have to cross to reach them? Or evaluating the possibilities for cover if they decided to make a run for it?

Whatever he was looking for, what he was finding couldn't be encouraging, she decided, scanning the expanse that lay between them and their mounts. Michael's rifle, in the saddle holster on the paint, might as well be on the moon.

"Michael?"

"We wait. From the way he set this up, I don't think this is his normal method of operation."

It wasn't, she thought. Not based on their one encounter. He must prefer dark, deserted streets and cold steel.

"Meaning what?"

There was a small hesitation before he answered.

"In a situation like this, whoever makes the first move is the one who blinked. We stay here, we keep our heads down, and we force him to come to us."

Instinctively, she applied more pressure to her injury, wincing against the pain, remembering that they hadn't bothered to take the water they'd brought off the horses. Like the rifle, it was tantalizingly close and yet so damn far out of reach.

Heat wasn't yet a problem, but eventually it would be. As would blood loss and dehydration. It seemed the only thing they could hope for right now was that their assailant was not any better prepared for a game of chicken than they were.

Chapter Eighteen

She had lost all sense of time. It seemed as if they had been hiding in the narrow shelter provided by the boulder for an eternity, although the position of the sun indicated that it was only midafternoon.

Michael had succeeded in drawing the assassin's fire a couple of times in order to check his position. That didn't seem to have changed. Apparently he wasn't ready to blink, and she wasn't sure how much longer she could wait for that. She was conscious of a creeping lethargy that frightened her because she was afraid she knew the cause.

"Nicki?"

She opened her eyes, shutting them quickly against the painful glare of the sun, which was directly overhead. Michael was leaning against the boulder, holding her head in his lap. With his left hand positioned beneath her shoulder he'd been keeping pressure on the wound. In the right he held the Glock.

"I need to talk to you," he said.

She put her hand up to shield her eyes, surprised at how much energy that simple gesture took. "What is it?"

"I don't think we can wait any longer. I'm going to leave you the Glock."

He had shown her how to use it during their first excursion. In case of an emergency, he'd said as he set up the targets. Although she had grown up around weapons, she had never before fired a handgun. He'd stood behind her, critically assessing her skills, until he was satisfied that she could hit the broad side of a barn.

"You're going after him?" she asked, struggling to prop on one elbow.

"I don't think we have any choice."

Because of her. Because of the injury. Given how rocky she felt, she couldn't argue with his assessment. Still, she didn't want him to leave her here alone. She fought off that childish cowardice and nodded her understanding.

"Okay," she said.

"You'll be fine. Just stay here and stay down. When I come for you, I'll call out your name. I'll give you plenty of warning. Anybody who approaches and *doesn't* do that, shoot them. You'll hear them coming."

"You need the gun," she said, realizing only now that if he left the Glock with her, he'd be facing her enemy unarmed.

"I'm going to get the rifle."

She turned her head, looking toward the horses. They seemed even farther away than they had the last time she'd looked.

By the time she'd completed that assessment, he had already started to move. Still keeping low, he had gotten his feet under him, one hand on the ground, like a sprinter preparing to leave the blocks.

It was all happening far faster than she was prepared for. She put her hand, the one holding the Glock, over his forearm.

"Wait."

Although she could tell this was an unwanted hindrance,

he obeyed. The turquoise eyes, which had also been focused on their distant mounts, returned to hers.

She could see a calm determination within them, but no fear. Of course, he had probably faced this situation dozens of times in the past. He had probably made his peace with the thought of death long before now.

She hadn't. Not her own. Not his.

"What are you going to do?" she asked.

"I'm going to kill him."

"Wait until it gets dark," she said desperately. She wanted to keep him with her, despite her growing doubt that she could last until nightfall. At least she wouldn't die alone.

"Right now, we know where he is," he said reasonably. "We won't have any way to tell that in the darkness."

"Michael."

She hated the pleading quality in her voice, afraid it might weaken his resolve. Intellectually, she knew he was right. Emotionally…

What she was feeling must have been revealed in her face. He leaned toward her, looking into her eyes with the same intensity as the first afternoon they'd spent together in her bedroom.

"I *can't* wait, Nicki. I have to do this now. Don't make it any harder."

She wanted to beg him not to go. She wanted to use her injury and her growing exhaustion to influence him against deserting her. Something in his eyes prevented her.

Since she'd met him, he had never asked for anything from her except her trust. She had to trust him now.

Deliberately she lifted her hand, freeing him. And then she nodded again.

He took one more quick survey of the gunman's location on the ridge, as if he were fixing it in his mind. Then his body tensed visibly as he made ready to begin a run that seemed nothing short of suicidal.

Seconds ticked by, and yet he didn't move. Just as she was about to question the delay, he turned his head again, his eyes locking with hers.

"I made a mistake in not telling my father how I felt. A mistake I never got a chance to rectify."

He was talking about the ranch, she realized. The Royal Flush. He had never told his father how much it meant to him, and because of that, or so he believed, the property had been given to Colleen. Forever lost to him.

She nodded once more, uncertain why he was telling her this now. Knowing only that it was something he needed to say.

"I promised myself I wouldn't ever do something that stupid again," he said softly. "Not about anything that important."

Her heart began to pound, driving blood through her ears in a deafening roar. Everything but his words faded from her consciousness, even the thought of the assassin on the ridge. Everything but the importance of what the man stooping beside her was saying.

"I love you, Nicki Carson. If we get out of this—"

He broke the sentence, leaning forward to put his mouth over hers instead. The kiss was hard, almost rough. And it was over before she had time to realize what it meant.

Then the coiled muscles of his body exploded into action. Dropping the weapon he'd handed her, she grabbed for him, frantic to keep him beside her. More so now than before.

The tips of her reaching fingers brushed the back of his shirt as he scrambled to his feet. They were still outstretched as he began his run toward the horses and the rifle. Still outstretched when the first shot stuck the ground in front of him, throwing up dirt at the tip of his boot in a miniature geyser.

As it hit, Michael changed directions without breaking stride, zigzagging across the expanse like a broken field runner. He was favoring the damaged leg, although it didn't appear to slow him.

Nor did the shots that continued to rain down around him. Before he'd crossed half the distance, she had already decided there was no way the barrage of bullets could miss him. Not all of them. No way in hell.

Michael staggered, and then seemed to gather himself, continuing to move forward by sheer force of will. It was obvious, however, that something was wrong. Obvious from his inability to make those swift changes of direction. Obvious in the lessening of his speed although, as she had watched each endless second of it, the run seemed to be taking place in slow motion.

Michael. Dear God, Michael.

Then, as explosively as it had begun, it was over. He reached the horses, wrenched the rifle from the holster and in the same motion dropped to roll under the belly of the paint. Between the bullets thudding into the earth beside them and a man crawling around between their legs, the horses had become thoroughly spooked.

She couldn't bear to watch, yet she couldn't force her eyes away from what was happening. The possibility that they would step on him before he could reach safety was very real.

The animals milled as if they were maddened, rearing against their constraints. Between the confusion of hooves, she caught a glimpse of long, blue-jean clad legs.

When the dust began to clear, she could see Michael crouched down behind the gray. He must be talking to them, she realized, watching the horses' frenzy ease. Surely if he had presence of mind to that, it must mean he wasn't seriously injured.

Please, God, she prayed, *don't let him be hurt.*

The rifle above him had gone silent. Since there was no longer a clear target, perhaps the gunman had decided to conserve ammunition.

Her attention had shifted to the ridge. Her eyes searched the irregular patterns of sunlight and shade cast by rocks and vegetation, trying to decide if any of them conformed to the shape of a man. Wherever he was hiding, he was well camouflaged.

Giving up, she turned her head to check on Michael. The horses were standing quietly now. Only the occasional stutter-step indicated their recent panic.

And there was no sign of the man who had been crouching on the other side of them only seconds before.

THE BULLET had grazed his thigh. Despite the heady rush of adrenaline as he'd made that run, he'd been aware of the gouge it had torn through fabric and flesh.

Maybe the thickness of the denim jeans had provided some protection, because, although it was bleeding sluggishly, everything seemed to be in working order. The blood not only wasn't of the spurting variety, it wasn't even close to the seepage from the wound on the back of Nicki's shoulder.

He needed to take care of their assailant and then get her back to the ranch. In that order and as quickly as possible, he told himself as he crawled along the base of the ridge. He was holding the rifle in both hands, using his elbows and knees to propel his body across the rocky ground.

The assassin hadn't taken any more potshots after that fusillade while he was crossing between Nicki's hiding place and their mounts. Apparently he wasn't in a position to be able to follow Michael's movements here, at least not as long as he stayed on his belly. Or, and this was something he didn't want to think about, the gunman could now be on the move himself.

He should have told Nicki to fire off a couple of rounds every now and then. She wouldn't hit anything—not at that range—but it might keep the guy in place until Michael could get up there to challenge him.

He was climbing now, the rifle held in his right hand, the left used for balance or to help pull him over obstacles. And he was hurrying, choosing to sacrifice stealth in the interest of speed. The quicker he got to the gunman, the less chance there would be that Nicki would get hurt again.

Just stay low and keep your head down, he urged her telepathically, wishing he'd taken time to say that once more. Instead, he had decided that he needed to get away before he made a lot of promises he might not be able to keep.

He slowed his forward progress, moving far more cautiously now. He was getting too close to the shooter's location to take the chance that he might inadvertently warn him. From below, he had picked out a wind-gnarled pinon pine to use as his guide. It was now less than twenty feet above him.

He glanced below, locating the boulder behind which Nicki was hidden. From up here, it looked far too small to provide adequate cover, but he could only see what looked like part of her boot. At least she was keeping her head down.

As his gaze began to track back up the incline, it was drawn to something near the base of the slope. A movement? If so, it had been fleeting enough that he couldn't be sure of exactly what he'd seen. Maybe a flicker of sunlight striking something reflective.

Like the barrel of a rifle?

Unmindful now of the noise, he began to climb again, keeping an eye on the boulder below as he headed for the point he'd marked as the assassin's location. After only a few minutes he had found a position just above that spot so that he could see the entire area around the misshapen tree.

Just as he'd feared, there was no one there. With a total disregard for his footing, he began to descend the treacherous slope he'd just laboriously climbed. While he'd been up here hunting him, the assassin had been making his way down, headed toward the target he had intended to take out all along.

NICKI CLOSED her aching eyes against the sunspots that danced in front of them. The resulting darkness was incredibly restful.

Her head jerked as she started to doze off. Panicked at the possibility that she *had* been asleep, even briefly, she raised it to survey the area around her. Nothing had changed in what must have been the few seconds she'd had her eyes closed.

She shifted a little, trying to press the pad made from Michael's shirt more tightly against the wound on the back of her shoulder. The position she was forced to assume in order to do that was awkward and uncomfortable. And since the fabric was completely soaked with blood, she couldn't be certain the pressure was doing that much good.

She started to put her other hand under the elbow of the arm wrapped around her body and realized it was holding the Glock Michael had given her. Her fingers, wrapped tightly around its stock, seemed numb and unresponsive.

She loosened them, trying to stretch out their stiffness.

She wished she could manage to do that with the rest of her cramped body, but there wasn't enough room.

She turned her head, trying to find Michael on the rugged escarpment that loomed above her. Sunlight shimmered off the light-colored rocks. She blinked against it, not daring to close her eyes.

She realized she was no longer pressing the pad against her shoulder. She had begun to lift the hand that held the blood-soaked square when her attention was drawn to the horses. They were milling again, just as they had when Michael had slipped under them. She pushed herself upright, trying to see if he were again hiding behind them.

She thought she saw something moving through their shifting legs, but heat waves rising from the ground between them distorted the air. The scene wavered and blurred, making it difficult to distinguish exactly what was there. She blinked to moisten the dryness of her eyes.

When she focused on the horses once more, she thought for an instant that she must be experiencing some kind of flashback. Or a heat created hallucination. A man was running across that barren, empty stretch between the animals and the boulder where she was hidden.

Michael? Could it be Michael?

She tried to remember what he'd told her. Something about yelling out her name. Giving her plenty of warning.

There was no sound at all. No footsteps. No wind. Nothing. It was exactly like one of those silent movies. Flickering images with no dialogue.

No dialogue. And there was supposed to be. He had told her that.

She struggled to her knees, knowing that she no longer had any reason to worry about keeping her head down. She put both hands around the butt of the Glock, bringing it into firing position like Michael showed her.

Michael. What if this was Michael? What if he *was* yelling at her, and she couldn't hear him? Just as she couldn't see his face clearly enough through the sun-induced haze to make an identification.

She batted her eyes to clear her vision as the index finger of her right hand closed over the trigger.

Where the hell was Michael? Why wasn't he here to help her?

If this wasn't Michael, then the only person it could be—

She raised the weapon, pointing it like a finger at the center of the approaching runner's chest.

Don't get fancy, Michael had told her. *Locate the widest area of the target, point the muzzle and gently squeeze the trigger.*

God, he was so close. Almost here. Almost on her. Almost—

He had a gun, she realized. He was holding it out in front of him with both hands, pointing it at her.

Not Michael. Not Michael.

Her finger tightened over the trigger as she tried to remember everything he'd said.

Squeeze, don't jerk. Gentle pressure.

But he was so close. Too close.

The gun went off, although she wasn't conscious of having completed the pull. As it did, the muzzle jerked upward. She tried to control it, concentrating on lining it up again on the center of the target.

Although her brain didn't seem to be making logical connections, she understood that she must have missed because he was still coming. She fought her shaking hands, trying to keep the big gun from wavering.

The running man skidded to a stop in front of her, his boots sliding over the rock-strewn ground. She had time to know that she had never seen him before in her life before the muzzle of the gun he held out in front of him began to lower. Although her hands still trembled as they tried to line up the Glock, his seemed rock steady.

The black eye of the weapon he held was pointed directly between her eyes. It was the one thing in the shifting kaleidoscope of images that appeared stable. Unambiguous.

She could even see his finger moving, tightening over the trigger. Squeezing it ever so gently. Just as Michael had tried to teach her.

The sound of the shot seemed to come from a great distance, her own a fraction of a second behind it. She didn't think she had managed to get the muzzle aligned with the center of his chest, but as she watched, the gunman seemed to hesitate.

His mouth opened and then closed, and his eyes widening in shock. The gun he held began to lower until it was no longer pointing at her forehead. And then, no longer pointing at her at all.

When it finally went off, the bullet plowed into the ground at his feet. A finger of dirt kicked up, as if someone had scooped it out and thrown it into the air.

In slow motion, his knees began to bend forward. He didn't release the weapon, not even to put his hands out to try and stop his fall.

His forehead hit the ground last, bouncing as it collided with the ground. That, too, produced a small cloud of particles that lifted into the still air before they settled to earth again.

Throughout the entire sequence she had kept the Glock trained on him, the barrel following his slow descent. It took her a moment to realize that he was no longer moving. Another to understand that the threat he had represented was ended.

Still she held the gun pointed at him. Afraid to move.

Afraid that if she did, he would come back to life. That he would raise the weapon that lay under his body and gently, ever so gently, squeeze the trigger again.

Again.

Ridiculously, she looked down, trying to see where the bullet had struck her. There had been no pain. No force of impact. Not like before. Which meant...

Gradually she came to the conclusion that whatever had happened to the bullet he'd fired, it hadn't hit her. She was alive, and she hadn't been shot. Not this time.

She took a small sobbing breath in celebration. As she did, she became aware that someone was running toward her, boots crunching over the gravel with a sound she was by now too familiar with.

She lifted her head to face the new threat, setting off a violent wave of vertigo. The world swam out of focus, grew gray and then black. She struggled to bring it back.

The sun seemed blinding in its intensity. She brought her weapon up, aiming it at the sound of those running footsteps because she couldn't see anything but glare.

"Nicki?"

Her finger closed over the trigger as Michael's words echoed in her brain. *Gentle squeeze. Don't jerk.*

That's what she had done wrong before. That's why the muzzle had lifted. Hands shaking, she aimed at the silhouette moving across the sun-brilliance patch of open ground.

This time she'd get it right, damn it.

"Nicki!"

From a great distance, she recognized Michael's voice. He was calling her name. She wanted to tell him that she had to do this first. One last thing to do, and then maybe they'd let her rest. That's all she wanted. Just to lie down somewhere cool and dark, even if it was in one of Colleen's beds.

"Put it down, Nicki. Put the gun down. It's over. It's all over."

She concentrated on the movement of her finger over the trigger. Slow and steady. The figure before her was growing larger and larger, his darkness blocking out the painful light from the sun.

Just choose the widest point of the target…

She blinked again, narrowing her eyes against the glare. As she did, for a second the face of the man coming toward her was clear.

His mouth was moving. She realized she could even hear the words coming out of it. She had been hearing them for a few seconds now, but they had had no meaning until she put them together with his face.

Michael. Michael was calling her name. Just as he'd told her he would.

Her finger eased off the trigger. As it did, the strength in her arms seemed to evaporate. Still holding the Glock in both hands, she let her arms fall.

Very carefully she laid the gun on the ground. Then she put her palms down either side of it, head hanging. She closed her eyes, giving in to the pleasant darkness she had fought.

Michael caught her before she collapsed. As his arms closed around her, she opened her eyes, looking into his.

"I've got you," he said. "It's all over. I'm going to take you home."

She licked her lips, trying to gather enough moisture in her dry mouth to form the words. She couldn't do it. It was all too hard. Giving in to the exhaustion she'd fought for hours, she closed her eyes, concentrating on the promise he'd made.

Home. Finally, finally she was going home.

Chapter Nineteen

"They got a match on the fingerprints," Colleen said.

Even in the dim lighting of the hospital corridor, Michael could see that the furrows were back in her forehead. She had a right to them.

He had dumped everything into her lap as soon as he'd gotten Nicki back to the ranch. Colorado Confidential, with the help of the DPS, had taken care of the body of the man he'd killed. He had known they sent the assassin's fingerprints through the national database. He just hadn't had time to worry about the results.

He leaned tiredly against the gray tiled wall, prepared to listen. Before he gave her his full attention, however, he glanced down the hall to the door of Nicki's room. Shawn Jameson, looking big and powerful, was standing guard in front of it.

Reassured, he turned back to Colleen. "And?"

"His name was Joseph Delano. He's wanted in connection with the murders of two women in the Washington area."

A coldness settled in the pit of his stomach. Two women.

"D.C.," he clarified. When she nodded, he asked, "Do we know who they were?"

There was a small hesitation, but she told him, her eyes

compassionate. "They'd been implicated in the call-girl ring I told you about."

"The one Nicki supposedly belonged to?"

"That doesn't mean it couldn't have been a setup."

Her face said she didn't believe that, although the suggestion had originally been hers. As far as he was concerned, there was no use discussing this until he heard from the people he'd asked to look into those allegations.

He had requested a down-and-dirty investigation, the kind that would turn up everything, no matter how cleverly hidden. How that was progressing was something else he hadn't had a chance to check on. Just as he hadn't had a chance to sleep or shower or do anything beyond worry.

He'd done plenty of that. Since it was a relatively new activity for him, he was finding it not only time-consuming, but highly unpleasant.

"And we finally got word from the CDC on the samples you provided. Apparently the blood contains an antibody for Q fever."

"Q fever?" Michael questioned.

"A bug that causes a deadly strain of flu-like illness. There's been some talk in the past about using it as a biological weapon. From the spraying you described at the lab on the Half Spur, I'm wondering if they're testing some kind of aerosol vaccine for it on the sheep."

"If someone in Gettys's position is involved in testing a biological weapon—even a vaccine for one…"

Michael let the words trail. The political ramifications of having a U.S. senator engaged in anything like that would be as obvious to Colleen as they were to him.

"Wiley Longbottom has suggested we investigate a flu with characteristics similar to Q fever that hit Silver Rapids about five months ago. Two elderly people died from it at

Gilpin Hospital in Denver. Shortly after that, the hospital's records room went up in flames.''

''And you want me to look into that fire?'' Michael asked, his concern for Nicki warring with his need to get to the bottom of whatever had been going on at the Spur.

''No, big brother, you're still officially on bodyguard duty. I'm assigning this one to Shawn. Not only is he screaming for something to do, he's an experienced arson investigator. And Fiona and Night are occupied following up the other leads we had on the Langworthy baby.''

''At least we know there's no baby at the Half Spur.''

That was about all he could be sure of about that operation. He didn't have any answer for the fire that had threatened Nicki. It could well have been just what Quarrels had suggested—an accident caused by Ralph's smoking. Or maybe someone had decided to issue a warning to whoever was poking around the secret activities on the ranch. Since Nicki had been seen by Johnson in the office, she would be a likely target.

He might never know the truth, he acknowledged, his eyes considering the closed door of Nicki's room. And at this point, at least as far as he was concerned, the more important consideration was simply keeping her safe.

''How is she?''

The concern in his sister's voice seemed genuine despite Nicki's conviction that Colleen disapproved of their relationship. He didn't give a damn whether she did or not, of course, but since he was going to need a safe place to take Nicki after the doctors released her, maybe this would be a good time to clear up any misunderstandings.

''She's going to be okay.''

Saying the words out loud brought an unexpected ache to the back of his throat. Even he could see how much improved Nicki was today—stronger, more alert and very anxious to get out of here. Which brought him back to what he needed to say to Colleen.

"I want to bring her to the ranch."

"Of course," his sister said quickly. "I told you that the Royal Flush is as much yours—"

"And whatever you feel about the assassin's connection to the call-girl ring, I don't want you to reveal those feelings to her. Not by word or action. Not by thought if you can help it. Keep whatever doubts you have to yourself, Colleen, because I promise you Nicki wasn't involved."

"Then you've heard back from—"

"Not yet, but even if they tell me…" He took a breath, thinking how far he had come from those first doubt-filled days on the Half Spur. "That's something I know, no matter what they tell me."

"But—"

"Like you said. There's such a thing as personal judgment. I've made mine. It isn't subject to change."

He had realized that while he'd waited through the surgery. Waited alone because everyone else had been busy taking care of Delano's corpse. And he owed Colorado Confidential, and especially Colleen, a huge debt of gratitude.

"Please believe that I only want what makes you happy," she said stiffly.

He nodded. "I know."

"And you're saying she does? Despite—"

"Despite everything," he said.

It was probably just as well his sister didn't understand that any glass walls he owned had been stoned long ago. Her eyes searched his before she nodded.

"Call me as soon as you know when they'll release her. Oh, and that reminds me. Someone called for you this morning. They left a number. No name, no message, just this," she said, taking a sheet torn off the message pad in her office out of the pocket of her slacks.

He glanced at it before he wadded it up in his fist. "Would you do one more thing for me?"

"Something more challenging than disposing of a body?" she asked, smiling at him.

"Not even close. As a matter of fact, I think you might just enjoy this one."

HE PUNCHED the number on the paper Colleen had given him into the hospital pay phone, then turned so he could see the door to Nicki's room. He could have asked Jameson to stay, but this was a call he preferred to make in private. Despite what he'd said to his sister, he wanted a few minutes alone to digest the information he was about to be given.

There's such a thing as a personal judgment. I've made mine. It isn't subject to change.

The words echoed in his head as he listened to the distant ringing. After the fourth or fifth ring, he was ready to hang up. More than ready, he realized. He was relieved.

He had already taken the receiver away from his ear when someone answered. He brought the phone back up quickly, aware of a slight tremor in the hand that carried it.

"You asked me to call," he said into the mouthpiece.

"You're a hard man to get in touch with," the man on the other end of the line said. "I took a chance your sister might know how to reach you. The number you gave me seems to be out of service."

The satellite phone. Michael couldn't even remember where it was. He hadn't thought about it in the long days he'd spent haunting this corridor and the surgical waiting room upstairs.

"Sorry. We had some excitement."

"Yeah? I heard the D.C. police just cleared a couple of murders they've had on the books for almost a year. That have anything to do with your excitement?"

"It might have," Michael acknowledged.

Apparently the identification of those prints had triggered an official request for information, which the DPS had shared with the cops. He hoped that sharing had been reciprocated.

"If I'd known you were going to go off on your own," his former colleague said, "I wouldn't have worked so hard on getting the stuff you asked for." Despite the admonishment, there was a thread of amusement in the deep voice.

"It wasn't something I planned," Michael said truthfully.

"You never did, as I remember. Things like that just seemed to happen whenever you were around. So, you still need the information?"

Michael toyed with the idea of saying no. It couldn't matter what this man had found. What he'd said to Colleen was nothing less than the truth. How he felt about Nicki wasn't subject to change.

If that's true, then what's the danger in hearing it?

After all, there might be other things that he needed to know in order to protect her. Other people involved besides the man he'd killed. Until he had all the facts, he wasn't in any position to know what he needed to guard against.

"Give me what you've got," he said.

He closed his eyes, leaning forward so that his forehead rested against the cool, slick surface of the tile. For the first time he was conscious of a dull ache at the back of his neck and in his shoulders. Tension or tiredness. He turned his head from side to side, willing the muscles to relax.

"The women Delano is suspected of killing were prostitutes, only when they frequent the elite circles those two operated in, I guess you don't call them that. There was some heavy capital backing the ladies, enough to get them invited to private parties given by both sides of the aisle. Their job was to troll for any of our representatives who might have a wandering eye. From all accounts they had everything they needed to attract attention—looks, style, intelligence. The ability to be all things to all people."

"I take it they were successful," Michael said dryly.

"Lots of guys up here think power bestows sexual prowess. Old goats buy into their kind of flattery because after all, they chair a frigging big committee. Why shouldn't some twenty-something be interested in them? So yeah, you could say they were successful."

"And that's what got them murdered?"

"I don't know what got 'em murdered. Maybe they were *too* successful. Or maybe they weren't successful enough."

"Meaning?"

"They weren't working alone, and the blackmail wasn't of the financial variety. More in the way of influence brokering. Vote right, Senator, and the pictures of you wearing a whip and nothing else won't get sent to your wife or your constituents. There were probably a lot of our esteemed legislators who didn't grieve when those two turned up dead. That doesn't mean they were in on the killings."

"What about Delano?"

"He's got a long record of arrests, but no convictions. Good lawyers from a firm that represents a number of mob honchos. Delano seems to have had some slight past association with one of them. Somebody named Helio DeMarco. From everything I can find out, however, DeMarco wasn't involved in the call-girl operation."

"Maybe somebody got tired of having his balls in a vice."

"And so they hired Demarco and company to loosen the tension? It's possible. The men who were caught in that blackmail aren't the kind who would enjoy rolling over. I can see one of them deciding to fight fire with fire. They had a lot at stake."

"Was Franklin Gettys one of them?" Michael asked.

He had passed the name on when he'd set this into motion. Nicki was convinced Gettys was behind the attempts on her life, but he couldn't see how the incident she'd described tied to what he was hearing now.

"Gettys is always trolling, but he fishes in his own stream. And he makes sure there are plenty of pretty young things swimming around him to take the bait."

"You're saying he wasn't being blackmailed."

"Not that we could discover. That's not to say it isn't possible."

If the people he'd put on this couldn't discover a connection between Gettys and the women who were killed, Michael would be willing to bet there wasn't one. That didn't preclude him from having any connection to what was going on, however.

"How about Gettys working from the other end. Helping to entrap his colleagues."

"Gettys is one of my favorite assholes, but he doesn't seem to be involved in this, Mike. Not from either direction. The only interesting part of the Gettys question is the intern."

A now-familiar coldness stirred in Michael's stomach. He had been trying to concentrate on the information and had deliberately avoided asking about Nicki. It seemed there was no longer any way to put that off.

"Nicola Carson," he said, his voice controlled.

"A latecomer to the party, by the way."

"Latecomer?"

"I'm not quite sure how her name got tied to this in the first place, but that didn't happen until after the murders."

With his left hand, the one that had been pressed against the tile, Michael pushed away from the wall. His heart rate had accelerated because he believed he knew where this was going. He glanced down the hall toward Nicki's door again before he asked the vital question.

"Are you saying she wasn't part of the prostitution setup?"

"Any compromising situations Carson might have gotten involved in were all private. And they sure didn't make the papers. She had couple of boyfriends since she's been in town, none of whom were in positions of power, and they sure didn't take her to the events we've been talking about. Before that, she was a scholarship kid who grew up poor and ambitious. She wanted out, but she didn't take any shortcuts to do it. She went to school, worked hard, kept her nose clean and got some attention from the right people. She *did* work for Gettys, which set off alarm bells, just because Franklin's the scumbag he is. She's never been seen in his company socially, however, and there were no calls from him to her home or cell phone or vice-versa."

"You're saying she wasn't involved in any of this," Michael said flatly.

The tension seemed to have drained from his body as his friend talked. He fought the urge to lean against the wall again.

"As far as entrapping senators? Pure as the driven snow. She isn't clean as far as people connecting her name to it. Apparently that's why Delano targeted her."

"So how did she get tied to the scheme?"

"Mistaken identity maybe. There was an Elaine Carson who ran with a couple of the women who were involved.

She was a good friend of the first victim. Or Nicola's name could have surfaced some other way.''

"Like what?'' Michael asked.

"You want to hear what I know or what I think.''

"I'll take both.''

"I think somebody mentioned her name to the wrong people, and that was obviously done after the fact.''

After the deaths of the two women. "To set whoever killed the others after her?''

"Since that was the effect, you could assume that was the intent.''

An axiom he'd heard innumerable times in intelligence work.

"She pissed someone off, and so they made her a target?'' Michael asked, wondering if Gettys was crazy enough to do this because Nicki saw something in his office that he didn't want her to see.

"Or it was an accident. Confusion with the other Carson. There's always a ton of gossip in this town. We thrive on it. Somebody mishears a name, one that sounds familiar because it is familiar, but only in a different context. They repeat it to someone else and it goes from there. It could have happened in a dozen ways.''

"What about the other women in the scheme? The ones who didn't end up dead?''

"They seem to have done what Carson did. They're lying low somewhere. That's another thing that argues against her involvement, by the way. Most left town after the first murder. Within hours after the second one, they were all gone. Smart enough to figure out that the killing of one of them might not have been random. Two meant there was a contract. Nicola didn't leave after the second death, however. She was still in town for at least a couple of months.''

And given her response to the first threat on her own life, the attack in the Metro station, if Nicki had had any connection to the murdered women, she would have been gone. She hadn't left Washington because those deaths hadn't meant anything to her. Not on a personal level.

"And nobody can remember hearing about Carson's involvement with this until *after* she was gone," his friend said. "Her name hadn't surfaced in connection with the blackmail. Maybe when she disappeared somebody put two and two together and got five. Or maybe the story was a cover-up for what really happened to her. I don't suppose you're going to tell me what that was, are you?"

"Delano tried to kill her. She escaped."

"And hid until he found her again? That's what? Eight, nine months? Maybe we should hire her."

Delano had found her again, however, which seemed to lead back to the Half Spur and Gettys.

"By the way," his friend said as he was arriving at that point, "we're not the only ones demonstrating an interest in Nicola Carson lately. A couple of people I talked to said some reporter's been asking questions. *And* within the last couple of weeks. A Jeremy Canton. You know him?"

"I've heard the name," Michael said.

He had, of course. Colleen had asked Canton to check into Nicki's connection to the call-girl ring. It seemed he'd done so.

"He's been asking about the source of the original story—that Carson was connected to the murdered women. Said he was asking for a friend. I don't know if that's important, but I can tell you that it made people more cautious in answering our inquiries than they would have been if he hadn't gotten there first. They were real wary as to why they were being questioned, not once but twice, about a missing intern."

In Washington, having people asking the same questions about any criminal activity tended to create paranoia. Maybe Canton had asked the right people, or maybe...

The thought was sudden, but with it, a lot of things fell into place. If Canton let slip on whose behalf he was asking, it was possible that whoever had planted that story could have traced Nicki to the Royal Flush through the inquiry he and Colleen had set in motion. *Son of a bitch.*

"That's all I got," his friend said, unaware of the possibilities he'd just opened up. "Nicola Carson wasn't involved. I can't tell you definitively how her name got tangled up in that mess. And I don't see anything that connects the murdered women to Gettys, either. I think that's all you asked about."

"Any idea who hired Delano?"

"Not a clue. Somebody who has mob contact, obviously, but that doesn't eliminate all that many people."

"Some congressman or senator who was being squeezed."

"That would be my guess, but the field's wide open. We don't know all the people who were blackmailed. We know who went to the police, but they're not the ones out hiring hit men. Those we don't know."

"I owe you," Michael said.

"Buy me dinner the next time you're in town. I have expensive tastes."

"Done."

"Take care," his friend warned. "However innocent Nicola Carson may be, she's been judged guilty in the court of public opinion. The people who were stung in this operation are used to getting their way and be damned to anyone or anything standing in it."

"I'll remember that."

He would. There were still too many loose ends to be

complacent about having taken care of Delano. After all, he had almost let the bastard kill Nicki. The next one who tried might have better luck. Or better aim.

HE EASED THE DOOR OPEN and stepped into the darkness of the hospital room. After it closed behind him with a pneumatic wheeze, he stood in the darkness listening to the soft pings and beeps of the monitors. They were almost comforting.

"I missed you," Nicki said.

His eyes hadn't adjusted enough to realize she was awake. He walked over to the bed, where there was more light from the machines, and kissed the hand she held out to him.

"Some business to take care of."

"Anything I should know about?"

"I was returning a phone call to an old friend."

It took a second or two for her to understand the veiled reference. He wasn't even sure how he knew when she had. Maybe a change in the tension of her fingers, still held in his.

"So now you know," she said softly.

"It's been a long time since I cared."

She nodded, seeming to accept that. "Have you told Colleen?"

"I told her I was bringing you back to the Royal Flush. I haven't talked to her since I made the call."

"Did he tell you anything that makes sense of all this?"

"Maybe. Some things that helped, anyway. The man I killed was wanted in connection with the murders of two women involved in the call-girl ring. My source thinks his targeting you may have been a simple case of mistaken identity. An Elaine Carson *was* involved with some of the principles. Maybe someone got the two of you confused. It could have happened in any number of ways. Maybe something as simple as you working for a senator and they were targeting them.''

There didn't seem any reason to mention the other possibilities his friend had suggested. Not yet. Maybe when she was stronger.

''No connection to Gettys?''

''None they could find.''

''If it had been there, you believe they would have found it?''

''They're good at what they do.''

She nodded, her eyes unconvinced.

''He's dead, Nicki. It's over. No matter why he came after you, he can't hurt you anymore. I promise you that.''

She nodded again, seeming to accept what he said, maybe because there was no other choice.

''Remember the first day at the ranch?'' she asked.

''On the Half Spur?''

Her lips tilted into a slow smile. It had been an eternity since he'd seen that.

''At the Royal Flush.''

The first time they'd made love. In a dim bedroom with the scent of lavender around them.

''I remember,'' he said.

''I asked you to hold me. To keep the nightmares away. I know the nightmares are over, but...I'd still like you to hold me while I sleep.''

''They probably wouldn't approve,'' he said, tilting his head toward the door behind him.

''*They* haven't been shot.''

''Do I detect a play for sympathy?''

''What you detect is a proposition.''

''I'm not sure that's a good idea,'' he said, despite his

immediate physical response to the suggestion. She was far too fragile.

"Then just sleep beside me. No one could possibly object to that," she said, still smiling at him. "Not even you."

"It seems to me that's what you said the first time you lured me into your bed," he said, answering her smile. "It didn't turn out quite that way."

"Well, now we've had some practice. Maybe this time we'll get it right."

For the first time in a very long time, Michael thought as he watched her move over to make room for him in her bed, he had—finally—gotten it right.

Epilogue

"What kind of surprise?"

"I swear, you're like a kid at Christmas," Michael said.

"I thought that's what you wanted. Rabid anticipation. Are we going somewhere?" Nicki asked as, with his hand at the small of her back, he directed her toward the living room.

He could understand why that would be appealing. He wished like hell they could. Neither of them had been off the ranch since she'd been released from the hospital.

He hadn't wasted the time they'd been housebound, however. The Royal Flush was now as much a fortress as money and expertise could make it. Security cameras had been installed and fed their information to monitors in the basement surveillance room. He had also had an invisible electronic fence put in that would warn him when anyone approached or left the compound. Anybody attempting to sneak onto the ranch now would have a much harder time than Delano had.

And as much as the two of them had enjoyed their rides to the outskirts of the property, those had been curtailed until this was behind them. He had undertaken to guard Nicki. Now that he knew Colleen's inquiries might have provided a link to this location, he wasn't taking any chances.

"Just to the living room," he answered, ushering her through the central room with the bar and old Dora's portrait.

"You are being *very* mysterious."

"Old habits die hard."

"Is this some kind of undercover assignment?" she asked with a laugh.

"You could say that." He opened the door, stepping back to allow her to precede him into the room.

He knew the exact moment she became aware of the surprise he'd arranged. Her forward progress stopped, and then she glanced at him over her shoulder. Her eyes were bright with tears, but he had no doubt they were tears of joy.

"Mom?" she said, turning back to the woman standing on the other side of the room.

Before the word was out of her mouth she was running into the arms of Terri Carson. Their embrace was almost difficult to watch. Although he was learning, under Nicki's tutelage, that expressing how he felt was acceptable, he hadn't yet reached the point of being comfortable with this much emotion. Not even if it was happiness.

He met Colleen's eyes and nodded his thanks. She was smiling broadly, obviously as pleased as he was.

He wasn't sure she would be successful in carrying out the favor he'd asked that night at the hospital. Nicki had tried to phone her mother before the attack on the Royal Flush only to discover that her mother's number had been changed and she was no longer listed with information.

They had speculated that was the result of the relentless press interest in Nicki's disappearance, but they couldn't be sure. Colleen had used her contacts to track her down and bring Terri here, all in secret, of course.

"Thank you," Nicki said, turning to smile at him through her tears.

"Thank Colleen. She's the one who located your mom."

Although the tension between the two women had eased since he'd brought Nicki home from the hospital, there had been a residual strain. Nicki put her arm around his sister, squeezing her tightly, although she was still holding on to her mother's hand. It was as if she couldn't bear to let her go, not even for a second.

He couldn't blame her for that. Her life had been ripped away from her through no fault of her own. Just to get back a part of it by being reunited with someone you love—

Someone you love. The words reverberated as he watched the two women in his life embrace, that annoying lump back in his throat.

"Mother, I want you to meet someone," Nicki said, using the hand she held to bring her mother to where he was standing. "This is Michael Wellesley. Michael, this is my mom, Terri Carson."

Nicki's mother extended her hand. As he took it, he realized the very shape of the bones as it rested in his was familiar. Just as her face was a reflection of her daughter's.

This is what Nicki would look like in twenty years. The elegant bone structure essentially unchanged, the tautness of the skin softened around the eyes and chin. Still beautiful. Still Nicki.

"How do you do," he said, feeling almost idiotic with the formality.

"Much better now, thanks to you," Terri said.

He returned her smile, relaxing a little. For the first time he realized how Nicki must have felt being introduced to Colleen.

"It was my absolute pleasure," he said truthfully.

"Until you have children of your own, you can't imagine how terrible it is, knowing that one of them is in danger and not being able to do anything about it."

Children of your own. The words had the same incredible

force as the others, especially as he visualized his fingers drifting over the contours of Nicki's body. Touching the place where she would carry his babies. *His babies.*

"She's safe here. I promise you that."

"As long as she has you to look after her," Terri said.

"Mom." Nicki's protest was soft, but her cheeks had colored becomingly.

"I intended to," he said. "Just as long as she'll let me."

Nicki's eyes locked on his, searching them. Whatever she saw there must have been what she was looking for.

She released her mother's hand and put her arms around his neck. Despite the presence of the other two women, Michael responded by enfolding her carefully in his arms, mindful of her injury.

After a moment she pushed far enough away that she could see his face. "If you're really leaving that up to me," she said, "you can make it forever."

He wasn't a man who made commitments lightly. And once he made them, he wasn't someone who ever walked away from them. He wouldn't from this one.

"Then...forever it is," he said softly, and was rewarded by her smile.

* * * * *

*Don't miss the next exciting installment in
the COLORADO CONFIDENTIAL series*
SPECIAL AGENT NANNY
*by Linda O. Johnston
Coming in September from Harlequin Intrigue*

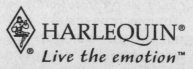

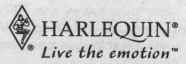

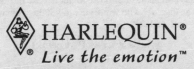

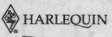
HARLEQUIN

INTRIGUE

COMING NEXT MONTH

Visit us at www.eHarlequin.com